American Indian Literature and Critical Studies Series
Gerald Vizenor, General Editor

THE MASK MAKER

The Mask Maker

UNIVERSITY OF OKLAHOMA PRESS · NORMAN

A NOVEL Diane Glancy

ALSO BY DIANE GLANCY • NOVELS • *The Man Who Heard the Land* • *Fuller Man* • *The Closets of Heaven* • *Flutie* • *Pushing the Bear* • *The Only Piece of Furniture in the House* • SHORT STORIES • *The Voice That Was in Travel* • *Monkey Secret* • *Firesticks* • *Trigger Dance* • ESSAYS • *The Cold-and-Hunger Dance* • *The West Pole* • *Claiming Breath* • POETRY • *The Stones for a Pillow* • *The Relief of America* • *(Ado)ration* • *Boom Town* • *Lone Dog's Winter Count* • *Iron Woman* • *Offering* • *One Age in a Dream* • DRAMA • *War Cries*

Text design by Gail Carter.

The paper in this book meets the guidelines for permanence and durability of the Committee on Production Guidelines for Book Longevity of the Council on Library Resources, Inc. ∞

VOLUME 42 IN THE AMERICAN INDIAN LITERATURE AND CRITICAL STUDIES SERIES.

LIBRARY OF CONGRESS CATALOGING-IN-PUBLICATION DATA
Glancy, Diane.
The mask maker : a novel / Diane Glancy.
p. cm — (American Indian literature and critical studies series ; v. 42)
ISBN 978-0-8061-3400-0 (cloth)
ISBN 978-0-8061-9194-2 (paper)
1. Mask makers—Fiction.
2. Indian women—Fiction.
3. Women artists—Fiction.
4. Oklahoma—Fiction.
I. Title.
II. Series.
PS3557.L294 M37 2002
813'.54—dc21   2001035862

MYSELF

My FACE IS SILVER WITH WEIRD SHAPES

OF BLACK. *I have long white whiskers.*

MY Nose IS VERY BIG. I FEEL SCARY.

I can run very fast. I WANT TO TEAR

SOMETHING APART.

Kara Rowden

THE MASK MAKER

Behold, a company of Ishmaelites from Gilead,
with their camels bearing balm and myrrh,
going down to Egypt.

Genesis 37: 25

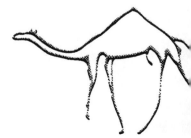

The Road

Edith was a mask maker. She traveled for the Arts Council of Oklahoma. She felt she was an artist in a place without art. A misfit in a practical world. But art was truth. It was revenge. It was masks that held Edith on the road. She had a car full of them. The masks told a story. But Edith

YAWEH: Grace is the substance of story.
URSET: It is a presence without its mask.

In the Bear's House
N. SCOTT MOMADAY

hated words. Wobblers. That's what they were. Especially in the mouth of Bill Lewis, her former husband.

Edith worked presenting masks to a world that didn't want them. What was she doing on the road traveling between schools by herself? Maybe the masks kept her from being blown out like the last of the sun she followed.

Edith thought about the masks as she traveled. They were sticky as love—sticky as paint not quite dry, like glue that held her to her former husband. Always back to him. It was a world full of roads that dropped off the earth at the edge of town; then she was on her own. In her nothingness. Without Bill Lewis.

The edge of town was Pawnee, Oklahoma, a remote place by some railroad tracks no one knew about. Had she ever looked at it without a mask? Had she looked at herself? ◥

As Edith traveled, she heard the masks tell their stories:

Everything was broken. The masks got together. They decided they could stop the breaking. They could restore. They could move the world again.

The masks found the evil that was breaking the world. The masks took the evil in their mouths. They chewed. It had lumps like gravy not stirred. They swallowed. Evil growled from their stomachs, but the masks had no stomachs. Therefore, the evil was nowhere.

The masks started the motor of the world. They shifted gears. The world started with a jump. The world has been rolling through space ever since. Once in a while evil catches up from nowhere. But the masks keep the world rolling, and soon the world gets ahead again.

Edith felt the desolation of the road as she drove. The masks filled in the missing parts. *Bone upon bone,* as Ezekiel said. There were such enormous stories. How could she carry them across the road? How could she make the masks tell the stories without words?

The Queen of Indians

Edith was a vizard maker, a mask maker. She went to schools and presented her masks. She had the students make masks. Edith was Queen of the Masks. Except Indians didn't have a queen. If they did, she would be Queen of the Indians. That's what! But what would an Indian queen do? She would be a queen. She would have a throne. No, thrones. They would be the hills of Oklahoma (where they cropped up). She would have subjects. They would be her masks.

There were princesses, yes. Indian princesses were all over the place. But why was there no QUEEN? One queen could not rule all the different tribes anyway. No, there would have to be as many queens as there were different tribes (which differed vastly) and differing bands within those different tribes. There would have to be queens all over the place. As many queens as princesses. But Edith decided to ignore that fact. She would be the Queen of Indians. She would be the Mask Maker.

Once Edith had stopped for a hitchhiker with her car full of masks. He looked warily into the backseat.

"Is it safe?"

"I make masks," she had told him. "I'm an artist for the State Arts Council. I have to do something with them. Halloween comes only once a year."

He had ridden with her, getting more *masky* as they traveled. She had told him to get out at the next town.

Residency

Every Sunday, Edith opened her map to find the Oklahoma town where she was headed for the week. Benjamin, her youngest son, helped her load the boxes of paints and brushes and masks into the trunk. Christopher, the neighbor's large dog, barked and came running, the neighbor calling, *Christopher! Christopher!* after him. One mask was not yet dry. Edith saw the blue paint on her finger. She took the mask from the box and put it in the front seat. The rest she hung on a rack across the backseat as if they were children.

Edith looked at her masks. She looked at her watch. She pushed away Christopher, who was standing on her foot, wagging his tail, thumping it against her.

"She'll be back," Benjamin said.

Edith hugged him until he pulled away. She closed the trunk of her car and drove off.

At the corner of Nash and Fourth, she waved at Maybelle, her former mother-in-law, who was turning onto Edith's street.

Before starting across the prairie, Edith stopped in town for gas. A man, also filling his tank, looked at Edith. "Going somewhere?" he asked.

"My job is traveling," Edith answered. "Staying ahead of myself."

Edith paid for the gas and got into the car. Charlie, the attendant, stopped her before she left. Her handed her a couple of dollars. "Pay me when you get back."

She thanked him and turned west from the gas station. She followed the highway beside the railroad tracks, pushing the road map on the seat out of her way. This Sunday she was on her way from Pawnee to Lawton, in the southwest corner of the state. She knew the way.

The sun sat on the hood of the car as Edith drove across the prairie on a stretch of single-lane Highway 64 toward Interstate 35. She heard "Balm of Gilead" on the radio. Edith turned it OFF. It didn't matter that there was nothing on the land. She couldn't see it, even if there was, because of the sun. The light was a mask she followed.

As she drove, she thought of the way her father had rigged up a light, trying to finish a job at night. He was always there when she drove a hitchhiker she picked up, but wouldn't get out at the next town. J. McKennah had been a bricklayer who started jobs and didn't finish. Once a man had dumped a load of bricks from an unfinished job in their yard. *I'll get to it*, Edith heard her father saying. Edith hated words. They changed meaning; divided. Her father had been able to shift his words. He had made them true in one particular circumstance but not true in another. Edith remembered her mother and father arguing over words. Edith wanted to cover all the bare places. Or was it all the covered places she wanted to make bare? Maybe she was a bricklayer like her father when she made masks. But she wouldn't work with words.

Edith passed open land with some scrub brush, some one-story trees. She heard the trill of grasshoppers in the weeds beside the road as she passed. Why was it still hot, this late in the fall? She knew the earth was burnt after summer, the brown prairie grass tough as hide. Maybe soon there would be gray mornings filled with dew.

She left her two boys, Joseph and Benjamin, ages seventeen and fourteen, with Maybelle, her former mother-in-law. She left Bill Lewis, her former husband. She left a friend, Bill Bixell, but she called him Bix. One Bill was enough. So was one J. McKennah, her father, riding in and out of her thoughts.

Her life always had felt torn up, Edith thought as she drove, always in transition between places though she'd never lived anywhere but Pawnee, Oklahoma. Had she ever been at peace with herself? It was the same with Bill, her former husband. Bix, her friend, was settled in himself, but he could not hold her interest.

Edith always felt unrest over her inability to support herself. "But all you do is make masks," Bill had joked in front of the boys.

The masks swayed on their rack in the backseat. *Going somewhere?* What'd he think?

At I-35, Edith turned south. A sign read, *Oklahoma City 50 miles.* At least now she wasn't headed into the sun. She touched the mask again to see if it was dry. Once she held it to her face as a car passed. *A mask is a face when you have none.*

Just north of Oklahoma City, she took Highway 40 to the southwest. She imagined her father got out at the first tollbooth, but she knew he was still with her. If he had gotten out, he'd only be waiting again at the next stop.

"Do we breathe in heaven?" Benjamin asked, holding his breath.

"Let it go, Ben," Edith said.

"We have air tanks on our backs in heaven," Joseph told him.

"Joe—" Edith said.

"Who were they?" Bill Lewis was furious.

It was when Joseph had disappeared for a day but was found the next.

Soon it was nearly dark. The prairie was not flat in southwestern Oklahoma, but rolled with low hills and a few trees camped along the horizon. ◢

The next morning, Edith entered Eisenhower High School in Lawton, Oklahoma, carrying a box of paints and brushes. She went into an office marked *Principal Pofar*. A clerk pointed down the hall. Edith thought maybe she would find someone to carry in the rest of her boxes.

The art room was dusty, empty but for a few tables and chairs pushed to a corner. Edith was disappointed in the room. She stood there a moment before she sat the box on the floor. She pulled the tables to the middle of the room with a roar. She placed the chairs at the tables. She dusted them. IS THERE NEVER ANYONE TO HELP ME? she thought. She strung a rope across the front of the room on which she hung her masks. She looked at them a moment. No, there was no one to help her carry in the rest of her supplies.

The students and teacher entered as she finished her last trip from the car. She was out of breath. Disorganized. Not ready. Getting settled in a new school was hard. She lost her sense of purpose, momentum, and had to start again. Edith held the masks to her face. "The masks are wordless. You can make words for them. A mask can give you answers. Or you can leave them silent. That's the way I want them. No one talking in your face." Edith just wanted to get through the week. What else was there she could do? *What do masks do?* Joseph asked her once. She was still trying to figure that out.

One student cut out a cardboard mask of his father. War-painted it.

"Go to your room," he said to the mask.

"No," the mask answered.

"You're grounded. You can't talk. I haven't given you a tongue." The boy drove a wad of wet newspaper into the mouth of his mask.

The teacher watched.

Edith looked at the teacher. "You can reach a student through a mask."

"We're supposed to reach them through math and English."

Edith made a round mask and painted it white. "The moon. Not just any moon. The harvest moon," she told the students facing her, looking to her for the meaning of the class, for the meaning of the masks they knew they were supposed to make. She wanted the tables in a circle, but there were too many students, and she didn't want to interrupt her work to change the tables. She might lose their attention, not that she had it anyway. "The moon can be bright and round, or it can be thin," Edith told them, "but it can only be what it is in relation to another: the sun shining on it, or the place on earth from which it's seen, or the phases it's in, from a sliver to a full circle."

"The earth is that way, too," a girl said.

"The moon is a mask," Edith told her. "Round and white as—"

Another girl answered, "—nothing."

"What do you think?" Edith asked another student.

He looked at her as if no one ever asked what he thought.

Principal Potifar passed the art room and looked at Edith,

but she didn't notice. The teacher who sat in the room with Edith ignored her. The teacher was grading papers—doing her own work. Edith noticed.

What did it matter?

In the lunchroom, Edith was introduced to other teachers. She ate. There was small talk. The teachers' lunchroom was off to the side of the cafeteria. Through the door, Edith could see the noisy cafeteria line, the cinder-block walls of the large institutional room, the tables and seats that were one piece, almost like picnic tables.

"You got children?" one of the teachers asked.

"Two boys. They stay with Maybelle, my mother-in-law. Former mother-in-law. She's better with them than I am. My husband and I didn't get along, but she was worth getting married for. I can handle kids I don't know better than my own."

"My mother-in-law couldn't handle my kids," the teacher said.

"Bill, the boys' father, takes them sometimes. Bix, my friend, also keeps an eye on them."

The teachers went back to their conversation.

"It matters."

"You're asking."

"I could."

Principal Potifar talked with someone, possibly an assistant, in the corner. Edith watched them a moment.

In the art room, Edith made another mask. She placed a gauze over the student's face, marked an opening for a nose and mouth, and cut. She placed the gauze on the face again and spread it with plaster of paris. Other students watched. "Give them a name that's an action: *Uprooting the garden with your dirt bike. Blame it on your brother. Lying.* You know you can say anything in a mask," Edith said.

"I don't have a dirt bike," a student told Edith. "My dad can't afford it."

"And what is your mask doing?" Edith asked another student.

"It's singing to itself," the student said.

"What's it singing?"

"Balm of Gilead."

"I heard that on the radio as I drove here," Edith told the student.

"Where do you live?"

"In Pawnee."

"Is that in Oklahoma?"

"Northeast of Oklahoma City. My masks and I drove down yesterday."

"Why?"

"To be with you."

"Why would you want to come someplace like this?" the student asked, looking at the abandoned room that resembled a war zone.

"You haven't been anywhere?" Edith asked.

"Where is there to go?"

"Where would you want to go?"

"Nowhere," the student answered.

"Then make a mask to take you nowhere," Edith said. "Come back and tell me what it was like."

Edith saw the teacher frown and look away while she was talking.

"What are we supposed to do with those masks?" a teacher asked in the hall.

Joseph was six when he didn't come back from school. No one had seen him.

"You can come out from hiding in a mask," Edith told her.

After class, she wrote a note on the blackboard: *Could you mop the room or leave a broom? Thanks.*

Edith nodded at Principal Potifar as she left Eisenhower High School for the day, but he was preoccupied or looking past her. ◢

After school, Edith sat on the bed in her motel room. She was going to make notes of what she remembered from school. There was something about the wad of wet newspaper the boy had made; it seemed like his mask was eating the moon. Her mask was the moon. And the earth was eating it. She belonged to the wind but gravity pulled her back. Edith was going to think about the wad of newspaper, but she lay down and was soon asleep. Before she knew it, she felt the GULPING. In a dream, she walked through her house in Pawnee, the rooms changing shape as she walked. The rooms opened their mouths as if they were masks. The rooms could be as large as the Oklahoma prairie she passed on the way to Lawton. When the masks opened their mouths, there were other masks inside. GULP! The masks did not speak. They made animal sounds. They made a line-of-trees-on-the-horizon sound. They made star-and-planet sounds. It was language, but not human language. ◢

She had heard the masks before. Was it when Joseph was kidnapped for the night?

She had made a mask.

Who had him? she asked.

Bring him back to me, she said to the mask.

When Edith woke, it was nearly dark. She looked from the window and saw a cafe. She washed her face and crossed the street.

In Dothan's Cafe, Edith looked at the clock. It was 8:10. She sat at a table near the cash register. "Too late for the special?"

The waitress went to the kitchen. She returned, shaking her head. "He can warm it up."

They looked at her in the cafe, but not because she was J. McKennah's daughter. Two men at a side table were still watching her. Maybe because Edith looked groggy from sleep. Why hadn't she seen Bill Lewis as a mask for her father? Bill didn't lay brick, but he was always doing catch-up; he was always behind. She remembered the disappointment of marriage; how she had tolerated it until she lost respect for herself, always giving in, settling for what she didn't want to settle for. The anger was there; the love, also. If she found respect for herself, it would be on her own.

Edith looked at her fingers. She looked out the window, but nothing passed on the street. She looked around the cafe. The bright fluorescent lights on the ceiling drove her back into herself, away from the worn flooring, the old paneling, the Formica tables and chairs, the old menus in their shiny plastic covers. There was nothing to see inside the cafe either.

"You passing through Lawton?" the waitress asked.

"I work in the schools as an art teacher."

The waitress looked at her and nodded as if she understood. The people in the cafe still looked at Edith. It was because she was new. She fidgeted with the paper napkin. They would get used to her in Dothan's Cafe, but the first time in a new town was uncomfortable.

"The Arts Council of Oklahoma sends me to schools that request an artist. I work with the students." Edith felt the need to explain. After a short silence, Edith said to the waitress, "I'm here five weeks. Usually it's just one."

A bell rang.

The waitress said, "I know there's no art or music at school. My girl's in the tenth grade." The waitress went to the pick up window and returned with a plate. "Roast beef and mashed potatoes. Corn."

"I forgot to ask your name," Edith said.

"Mildred," she answered. "And yours?"

"Edith Lewis."

The waitress went to another customer. Edith ate the meal by herself. *Masked potatoes*, she thought. She looked up, somewhat self-consciously, as if her thoughts showed. "I'll probably see you tomorrow night," Edith said as she paid for the meal.

Edith crossed the street from the cafe in a fierce wind.

What if she had trouble sleeping? She usually woke as soon as there was light, but she had slept so long in the afternoon, she worried about waking in the morning if she didn't get to sleep. What if the masks kept her awake with their mumbling?

"The wind is blowing," she said to the man in the office.

"That's what it does here."

"I need a wake-up call at 7:00."

The man nodded and wrote it down.

Edith listened to the news in her room. There'd been a shoot-out on Interstate 35 near Moore, south of Oklahoma City. The reporter didn't know yet what had happened. A bullet had hit the Chapel of Love. Edith knew where it was. She had passed it on the interstate on her way to a residency in Purcell. For some reason, she had noticed it. It was like the place where she had married Bill Lewis when they eloped.

Edith chose four masks for the corners of the room. She placed another one on the floor, in the center, at the foot of her bed. She hung one from the ceiling light.

South.

East.

West.

North.

Earth.

Sky.

Then the seventh direction.

Wherever I am, is where I am.

Help me through this week.

Edith looked at the phone. Turned out the light. The neon blinked through the drapes. She heard another car arrive. The door banged in the next room. She heard laughter. She sat up, looked at the phone again.

She called the boys, though it would add to her motel bill.

"Ben, while I'm gone you and Joe lay those bricks around the tree where the grass won't grow. You fed the cat? Where's Grandma? No, I don't want to talk to her. If Joe was there, he'd come to the phone."

After she talked to Benjamin, she sat in the darkness of the room, lay back down. A tear fell from the corner of her eye. She put a mask over her face, soon took it off.

Edith could not sleep. Bill Lewis slipped into her thoughts. It was anger that stirred her. Not him, but her inability to handle her relationship with him. Always back to her. Why was marriage an adjustment on her part, not his?

She had to flush it all out now and then. The more disappointment Bill faced in his business, the more stylized his behavior. He turned in on himself. Edith could recognize other men who were not doing well. It was the way they talked, behaved.

Joseph was found a day later by a farmer driving on a country road.

"Abducted by aliens," Benjamin said later.

"Don't say that, Ben." Edith told him.

"It was a lady," Joseph said.

"What did she do, Joe?" Bill Lewis asked.

"Gave me some coke to drink."

"What did you do all night?"

"Slept, I guess."

Had Bill ever known himself, or only the idea he wanted to have of himself?

Edith got out her notebook and looked at the drawings for

masks she had made for Lawton. Her work had to spread over five weeks. Why did they want her so LONG? What would she do? How would she last? Just keep making masks? She felt restless. She wanted to make something. She thought of the Halloween party next weekend. What would she wear? What mask? She looked at the ones hanging in the motel room. She looked at the chest of drawers. There was a bag of Hershey Kisses she had bought at school. Some club was selling them. That was it. A Hershey Kiss! She opened the bag. She sat one on the corner of the chest. She sat on the bed looking at it. A silver tower on the edge of town. A space ship. She would go as a Hershey Kiss. She drew it in her notebook. She would wrap a frame with aluminum foil.

Edith still could not sleep. She wandered through her house in Pawnee in her thoughts and looked at the masks on her walls. Her house was a refuge, like one of the wildlife sanctuaries she saw on the road. She got up again but didn't want to get out her paints; most of them were at school anyway. She could drive into the prairie night. She could call Bix. She could call her former husband. She could call her sisters. But they would all be asleep and sound impatient and questioning on the phone; her former husband more than anyone, no matter how often he had woken her when he came in late at night.

She thought of looking at her notebook again. She turned on the radio, then turned it off because the words irritated her. But she thought in words, didn't she? Maybe she would *just think in masks.*

Edith sat on the edge of the bed awhile, then lay back down.

Somehow, Edith slept. The masks moved in her dreams. She wanted to see the ancestors. She wanted to see visions. She wanted to dream of another world, but she saw her own car on the highway. She saw the students who needed help. She saw her own fear of not being able to help. Her masks were a camel train going to Egypt. They carried spices, balm, and myrrh. They carried Joseph, whom his brothers had sold. What was that to her? Joseph had a coat. He was a leader; the stars had bowed to him. His brothers were jealous. Was she dreaming the worries she had for her sons, Joseph and Benjamin? Had she sold part of herself? Was it Joseph, her oldest son, she had failed? With a father like Bill Lewis and a grandfather like J. McKennah, how could he be different? Or was she the Joseph who was sold?

"What did the woman look like, Joseph?"

"She had black hair and a straight face."

"That sounds like your mother," Bill Lewis had said.

Edith sent her dreams upward, but they got trapped in her thoughts. Where were the spirits? Where were the VISIONS? For Edith, visions were full of determination to get her work done, her boys raised. She wanted to find SOMETHING MEANINGFUL TO DO WITH MASKS. Something her former husband would respect and not laugh at behind her back (sometimes in her face). The teachers also. *What was she doing here?* Edith knew they thought. Bill Lewis had needed her help. If only she could have earned something from her masks. It wasn't until later that Edith had gone to work for the Arts Council. She had let Bill down. She should have helped earn their living. What else could she do but work with masks? Give her a gun. She'd fire into the Chapel of Love. Full of promise and hope that collapsed like an old star.

She woke and lay in bed thinking about her dreams. Where had the spirits gone? Why didn't they talk to her? She thought again of Bix, her friend. She thought of her former husband, her boys, her mother-in-law. She thought of herself as a mask maker. She belonged to her masks; she lived in a mask maker's house. But she also belonged to the world-that-was.

In her dreams, her boys moved away from her. She was holding out her arms to them, but her hands were MASKS. What were they doing? She wanted to keep the boys in school. But what would they do in Pawnee? In Oklahoma? In the world? Wasn't that the struggle her former husband faced? What was there for him to do? In the end, she felt it got down to keeping them alive. She knew Joseph was careless in his truck, driving across fields, jumping ditches, taking potshots at signposts on county roads. Who knew what else the boys did?

Sometimes Edith thought her masks were the old world that moved independently of her. Her life was built on a different tradition now: Christianity. But it didn't mean anything to her either. She wanted to be a Christian, but Christianity got in her way. Edith thought of Bix still teaching Sunday school. She thought of the sermons on Joseph in Egypt. The minister in Pawnee had been stuck there for several weeks. For some reason, she liked to think of Joseph in the pit while his brothers talked about what to do with him.

In the barren motel room at night, Edith heard a car pass on the street. Someone slammed a car door, entered another room. What time was it? What bothered her? A television too loud? Or the silence?

When Edith thought of Pawnee, she imagined she was in her one-story house on the edge of the small town, on the edge of the Oklahoma prairie. The five rooms in Edith's house were workrooms, except for the boys' room. She thought of her masks hanging on the walls. They were assorted papier-mâché, paper, and cardboard handmade shapes. The masks weren't necessarily for wearing but were objects in themselves. She walked through her house in her thoughts.

She saw her bed with a star quilt. Above the bed was an old leather mask and a painting, *Two Wolves Cut the Buffalo Herd in Two*. She had found the painting at Pawnee Hardware, which

Bix owned. Masks covered the rest of the walls. They had faces of the sun, the northern lights—which she had never seen, a comet, the moon, a few stars. Over them a sign that read, *Places I Have Been*. One mask, with the face of a baby, hung near the ceiling.

The other bedroom was a workroom; there was a highboy against one wall, and a small bed. The room was cluttered with workboxes of small animal bones, bark, twigs, bricks, rocks, pinecones, devil's claws, dried weeds and wildflowers, feathers, and various other found objects. The walls were shelved with art books, newspapers, notebooks, paint jars, jars of brushes, scissors, pencils, duct tape, and wires strung across the room on which hung various masks and objects. Some of the masks had animal or human faces. There was one mask that was a floor plan; the nose was a table, the eyes were chairs, the mouth a closet with a tag that said, *one-story mask*. On a table by the bed, there were a few black-and-white photos of the boys, her parents, her sisters, and herself as a girl on a horse.

A small room off the kitchen was for her sons, Joseph and Benjamin, though sometimes Benjamin slept in the single bed in Edith's workroom. As Edith walked through her house in her thoughts, she saw Joseph and Benjamin sleeping. Where did Maybelle sleep when she stayed all night? Edith's bed, perhaps, or maybe she preferred the sofa in the living room. Odd, she had never asked. The sofa was an oversized leather couch you could sink into with your whole self. Bix had sold it to her. It had been in his family for years. It was a western-style sofa, made for a hunting lodge. It should have been surrounded with moose and deer antlers and heavy bentwood chairs.

"Your masks are crowding me out of the house," Bill said.

The walls of the living room were painted a flat Indian red. Edith's bedroom was dark orange. Her workroom, mustard yellow. The boys' room, turquoise.

There was a dead tree in the backyard. ◥

In the morning, Edith looked at the motel room, remembering where she was. She had had a busy night; she remembered a clutter of dreams, but they passed. She was in the bathroom when the phone rang for her wake-up call.

At school, the students halfheartedly cut out the cardboard and painted their masks. One student looked out the window. Another had his head on the desk. One wrote a note. Some talked. A Hmong student was the only one who responded.

Maybe Edith could advertise in the Enid, Oklahoma, newspaper that was delivered in Pawnee and surrounding towns. *Masks for sale.* Customers would buy her masks. She would quit her traveling job. Sure.

Edith tried for something in class that would get their attention. "My father was a brick mason," she said behind the blue mask that she had brought to Lawton in the front seat. "He made walls for houses and whatever would let itself be brick. When my mother died, he took his trowel and bricked up a headstone for her."

A few students listened.

"My mask is red as a prairie fire—as red as the inside of a toaster where the rows of wires are hot with electricity." Edith talked as she worked with her own mask. "Have you seen the strings of prairie fire at night?"

The students didn't answer.

"Have you seen the windy days the voice gets away—when it tries to say something to make a connection somewhere?" Edith continued. "Those days you know you are toast." She made two slices into her mask. "The two slots of your parents."

As Edith worked, she heard the helicopters from Fort Sill,

the army base. Sometimes the windows rattled from howitzer practice.

Edith thought how the helicopters were masks, their propellers turning until they were invisible.

She remembered the storms wrapped in the sky. The clouds her mother was afraid of, the large brown ones that looked like grocery sacks. They could rip with wind and funnel clouds. And what about the sack she cut up in school to make a mask to hide behind? What about it? The sky was not to be trusted. It looked clear, but by afternoon, on a hot day, she could feel the clouds. And what of the tail that sometimes came from it?

The earth and sky were fighting. The sky was brown as the earth; the earth blue as the sky should be, wrestling until she couldn't tell which was which.

As Edith gave the students time to work, she became lost in her own thoughts. She was a mask maker, but it seemed the masks were making her. Why did she make them? What had been her first mask? Not the grocery-sack mask—no, there was one before that. She had covered her face with her hand when she didn't want to be seen. Why? She had done well in school. She had her two sisters, her friends. Later, she had Bill Lewis calling her, giving her a ride to school; her mother glaring at her when they backed from the drive. Her mother had not liked Bill, but Edith kept riding with him. What if she had listened to her mother? Who else would she have married? Not Bix. No, not Bix. Wasn't there anyone else? Is that why she covered her face? Not from being seen, but from seeing? There were words again, moving her thoughts around.

Edith remembered in church she had heard "Balm of Gilead." It was rehearsal and she sang in the choir, but she didn't want to.

"There's a Balm in Gilead." But the kids would sing, "There's a bomb in Gilead."

"Did you go to choir practice?" her mother had asked.

"Yes."

"Did you learn the words?"

"Yes."

"If you're lying, the sky will get you."

"There's a bomb in Gilead to make the wounded whole." But a bomb left a hole. That word could be *hole* instead of *whole*. She knew there was a hole in herself when she looked. She hadn't known it then, but she did now. It kept letting her separate from herself. It was the masks that covered that split (that break).

Edith didn't like church. It was putting on a mask that someone else had made. She had to sing a hymn she didn't know, didn't want to know, hadn't learned, her mother watching, knowing she hadn't learned the words and had lied about learning them.

A helicopter brought her back from memory. Where was she? In school. Eisenhower High School. Where she didn't want to be either. What were the rest of the words to "Balm of Gilead"? She hadn't learned them. She just said she had. Maybe she would have liked them. Maybe she would have liked them later. She heard the song often enough. There was something in the words that appealed to some people. Something they could relate to. Otherwise she wouldn't hear it all the time. But it was church music.

Edith walked among the tables, looking at the halfhearted masks the students made; the teacher telling them now to clean up.

She remembered how she took off with Bill Lewis to get away from everything. They'd been married in a chapel beside the highway, not the one in Moore with a bullet hole in it, of course, but another one. Then they kept driving to Mexico for a honeymoon. But it landed her back where she was.

"That's why I make masks," she had told Bill Bixell, her friend. "They cover my face. Plain and empty of song."

Suddenly Principal Potifar was in the art room. The students were gone. "You left a note on the board yesterday? You wanted the room cleaned up?"

"I came into an empty room."

"The chairs and tables are here."

"Buried under dust."

"We don't use the room."

"The art room?" Edith asked.

"We think in practical terms."

"What's more practical than reaching a student?"

"You're a visitor to the school. You cut up paper bags— paint faces on them. You'll be gone next week."

"My residency is five weeks."

"What you want done to the room has to be requested through my office." ◣

"What's the special tonight?" Edith asked Mildred in Dothan's Cafe.

"Meatloaf," the waitress answered.

"That's what I'll have."

"How's it going at school?"

"I'm working with the students. Letting them make masks. There's a lot of students in Lawton. It doesn't look that big on the map."

"We've got an army base here," the waitress said. "We've also got refugees."

"I guess that's why I'm here five weeks. I usually only stay at a school a week."

"We got a lot of disruptions. Army brats. Refugees. The

newly enlisted." The waitress said this with emphasis as she wrote Edith's order. "We got lemon pie tonight."

"I saw the refugees," Edith told her.

"They're from Cambodia. Laos. Anyplace. Ask your students where they're from. Hardly anyone's from Lawton. They were born on army bases in Germany, or just about anywhere in the world." Mildred grabbed the pencil that fell from behind her ear. "You been to Mount Scott yet and the wildlife refuge?"

"No, but I saw the Wichita mountain range on the map."

"It's those hills northwest of town."

"It was dark when I drove in Sunday night. It takes awhile to get settled. I usually drive around after a few days."

"My daughter's in one of your classes."

"Which mask did she make?"

"I don't know."

"I'd rather have the chocolate pie."

Mildred looked at the pie shelf. "We're out."

"Lemon, then." ◢

After school the next day, Edith drove past the Fort Sill army base toward the wildlife reserve in the Wichita Mountains, about twenty miles northwest of Lawton. She passed several gates that said, *No trespassing. Fort Sill U.S. Military Rifle Range.*

She drove to Mount Scott, circling 2,400 feet to the top. The highest point in Oklahoma. Or was it Black Mesa in the panhandle? Whatever Mount Scott was, it was the throne of Oklahoma. She was the QUEEN. She heard the howitzers from the Fort Sill practice range. She watched the ground fighters from Altus Air Force Base, some thirty miles to the southwest. She scavenged for found objects to use in her maskmaking.

I look at the land and see faces there. She heard her own voice. She stayed on Mount Scott watching the sun disappear.

Then she sat in the dark as the moon came up. She was a grown woman (more than grown) and she worked with masks! What was wrong with that? Something was. She just didn't know exactly what. How could doing the only thing she could do make her feel so lonely? Was she just stubborn, refusing to try something else even though she hated it? But hadn't she tried (always failing)?

Edith thought about how the moon changed depending on how she looked at it. She could see it as the mortar her father used in bricking; she could see it as the bottom of a Hershey Kiss.

"Did the alien wear a mask?" Benjamin asked.

Maybe Edith was the alien.

Maybe she had abducted Joseph and not remembered.

Maybe she was from another place.

Didn't she feel like a stranger in her own family?

Where had she ever belonged?

Didn't the ancestors know where they were going out there in space?

Didn't she want to get back to where she had come from?

Tomorrow another day of the week would pass. If she just waited long enough, she'd be on the way back to Pawnee. But to what? Her life was in her migrations, her travels over the road. ◣

The next morning, Edith crossed the street. The cafe was noisy with conversation. A group of farmers laughed at a corner table. Edith was an outsider to them. She took several postcards from a dusty rack in the cafe. She looked at the photos of the Oklahoma prairie, the Indians, an oil rig. She wrote a postcard to her former husband, which she never sent.

"Who you writing?" Mildred asked as she brought Edith's plate to the table.

"My former husband."

Mildred read, "Dear Bill, There's red rock and green grass. A blue sky. A bird flying over. With love from Mount Scott. Edith." The waitress didn't know what to say.

"I never send them," Edith told her. "I know they don't make sense—isn't that the way a former husband makes you feel? Having parts that don't connect?"

"Why're you still writing to him?" Mildred asked.

Edith didn't answer. ◤

In the art room, the students made masks. Edith worked with the students. She saw the images of eyes and mouths and noses. The images of gauze and paint.

"If you haven't gone anywhere, make a mask called *moving.* If your mother is a waitress, make a mask from the pages of her lined, green order pad."

"My clerk said you were bothering her about your check," Principal Potifar said as Edith left that day. "You won't give her the information she needs."

A frog in her oven.   "What does she need to know?" Edith asked.

Exodus 8:3   "Social Security. Address."

"I thought I'd given it to her." ◤

On Friday morning, Edith looked at the finished masks. One mask had sheets from a green order pad on each side of the face as if hair. Another mask had paint running from the eyebrow, though it had dried. The masks were not done well, except for the order-pad face. Edith looked at them, disappointed. She wasn't sure what to say.

A student sensed her disappointment and said, "What does a mask have to do with—where I come from?" He stood awkwardly a moment before he left the room. "My dad's a farmer."

"Maybe a scarecrow," Edith said. ◤

Edith entered Principal Potifar's office. She looked at the clerk. "I usually get paid at the end of the week."

"I don't have the check ready."

Edith loaded her car at the motel—carried out the carpet bag with her things in it—the bag had also come from Pawnee Hardware; not off the shelves, but from the dusty back room where Bix kept a generation's worth of his family's belongings. Her boxes of paints and brushes were already in the car. She hung her masks on the backseat rack. She started back to Pawnee from Lawton with a sense of failure.

North of Oklahoma City, a storm blew over the road. Edith kept going. She had made masks for Sunday school when the boys were small. She had made masks for the walls of her house. What did they mean? Nothing except that she kept making them. What good was the imagination? Wasn't it evil *always* according to the Bible?

Edith drove through the rain, talking to herself at times, telling herself what she did wrong. At least the hot spell would be over after the rain. Indian summer. She didn't have to go back to Lawton. She could call Principal Potifar and tell him she was through. She could live without money.

What were the dreams she had in the night? She had dreamed all week. But last night she remembered she had dreamed she made masks for the cemetery, one for each grave. Bix was with her. He had written Jesus on the foreheads of the masks. She didn't object. *If only it was written in their own hands,* she told him. She remembered she had kicked him once in Sunday school. He kept sitting next to her and she wanted him to move away.

Where was she going with her masks? he had asked. Where she wanted, she answered. But she also was going where she didn't want to go. She would have to go back to Lawton; she had no other income.

"Is it easier than being married?" Bill, her former husband, had asked. She thought about him as she continued north on Interstate 35 through the rain. Yes, being married was harder. It was the hardest thing she had done. She remembered she had felt powerless. At least now she had her life in her own hands.

She thought again of Bix. He was satisfied with his life. He lived a way she couldn't. That was why she had married Bill Lewis. She had his restlessness, his will, his dissatisfaction. They had come back from the honeymoon in Mexico accumulating disappointment, disillusionment, bitterness.

By the time she turned east on Highway 64 toward Pawnee, the rain had stopped.

Maybelle Lewis

You were born on a Sunday in May. Your mother would have eight children. But you were the girl your father called to sit by him. You went to school in a yellow skirt with a bandanna on your head because the wind gave you the earache. You knew your numbers. You could read books. You got married and had Bennah, a daughter who died, and Bill, a son who could hold the stars between his hands. You took him to the field in your old truck and lay in the truck bed and watched the stars. There were so many, the sky was soft white as chalk dust, and the blackness only partly there. Bill held his hands up to the night sky, and there was a constellation between his hands; not in the sky, but there in the truck between his hands. Then you watched the stars fall from him. What he held sometimes looked like stars, but they were hollow and soon collapsed on themselves. You watched the light leave his eyes. Nothing could put it back. You had a daughter-in-law, Edith, who was his wife and not his mother, and you saw her expect the stars from him. More stars and more. You could do nothing but watch the boys, Joseph McKennah Lewis, then Benjamin, your grandsons, and know they, too, would be sold to a camel train going to Egypt.

Pawnee

"You boys didn't get all that brickwork done," Edith said.

Christopher, the next-door dog, barked as she unloaded the car. Joseph and Benjamin helped her carry in her stuff. She asked about their week, thinking mostly of her own. She felt divided again.

"When do I get paid?" Benjamin asked.

"When I do."

She felt the burden of her life with Bill, though they were divorced. They had passed on their disappointment and dissatisfaction to their boys. Joseph was angry. Benjamin was quiet, but he was always thinking about someplace else, always thinking of something out of reach.

Saturday was Halloween, and Edith remembered the Hershey Kiss. She made a frame that hung from her shoulders, which she covered with heavy-duty aluminum foil.

"Love is a spook on Halloween. I'm going as a Hershey Kiss."

Joseph and Benjamin helped her wind the aluminum foil over the frame.

"I love duct tape, but it would take too much to cover a kiss. The foil is delicate; you have to be careful not to tear it. I think duct tape is something like what space must be out there in the universe. Shoot—I'm going to need more aluminum foil. Joe, go someplace you can charge it."

"How will you sit down?" Benjamin asked.

"I won't."

"What kind of mask are you wearing for the Hershey Kiss?"

"My own face," Edith answered.

"That will scare them."

"I want to make something for Halloween. Not all that candy in a sack. I could melt those caramels and roll the apples in it."

"Me'un Grandma'll make it."

"You aren't going out?"

"Ben's staying in," Joseph said.

"What'd you do now?"

"Smarted off to Grandma. She grounded him."

"The tinfoil—" she reminded Joseph.

"Why're you always making this stuff? My friends come over here and laugh." Joseph left.

Edith and Benjamin were quiet while they worked in the kitchen, the walls of which Edith had painted a dark, brooding green. They melted the caramel and rolled the apples in it and laid them on waxed paper in the dark, brooding green kitchen. The caramel hardened in the pan before they used it all. The apples stuck to the waxed paper. Benjamin dropped one on the floor.

"This stuff's like cement." She looked angrily at the pan, still stinging from Joseph's remark. Her feet made stick sounds as she walked in the kitchen. "Oh yes, the floor is sticky also."

"Maybe Grandma can clean it."

"My mother-in-law can do anything. She doesn't even have to read the instructions. But she can't clean this pan." Edith threw it at the wastepaper basket. Missed.

"Why do you make all that stuff, Mom?"

"Because I have to, Ben—" Almost to herself, she said, "Maybelle can look a person straight in the face without a mask. But I have to make masks. Anything whose face is painted on." She continued cleaning the counter. "Do your friends laugh, Ben?"

"They come over here and look at everything—I don't hear them laugh."

"I'm sure Grandma does—when I'm not here—"

Benjamin didn't answer. He changed the subject. "I tried to carve my pumpkin. The mouth is crooked. The tooth fell off."

"I'll give the pumpkin a mask."

"Which one? The sun?" Benjamin asked too hurriedly.

Edith looked at the masks on the kitchen wall. "The sun has a hole in it. What happened?"

"I was hitting a ball."

"In the house? Benjamin—you're fourteen."

"You got enough masks around here. Why do you have all of them?"

"Your friends don't laugh, huh?" She looked at Benjamin. "I remember masks lined up in the window of Bixell's Pawnee Hardware at Halloween. We didn't have money to buy one, but I'd look at them. Maybe that's why I make masks. What do I want more than anything? To have a mask. When your father and I got married we went to Mexico on our honeymoon. I saw the masks there. All those colors—red, green, yellow—full of hope. I wanted to fly wearing a mask of the moon."

Benjamin looked at her.

"I just want to earn my living making masks," Edith said.

"They made me feel hot and sweaty inside," Benjamin commented.

"What do you want, Ben?"

"A honeymoon that lasts."

When Joseph returned, the cat ran through the kitchen. It was the first time Edith had seen her since she got back from Lawton.

"Where've you been?" Edith asked Joseph.

"Buying your tinfoil."

"It took long enough."

"I got other things to do."

They finished wrapping Edith's frame with Reynold's Wrap. She had a strip she fastened to the top of her head. Edith knew she couldn't get in her car in a Hershey Kiss costume. The bottom was too wide.

"Can you take me in the truck?"

"You can't get in it either," Joseph answered.

"I'll stand in back."

"Can't you walk?"

"I can't walk six blocks through Pawnee dressed like this," Edith said.

"But my friends can see me driving a Hershey Kiss through town?" Joseph asked. "How will you get home?"

"Someone will bring me."

"Probably Bix," Benjamin said.

As they left the house, Maybelle, Edith's former mother-in-law, drove up.

"You got your own house to watch tonight," Edith told her.

"I thought maybe your masks needed taking care of. I left on my recording of the barking dogs. Joseph stopped by. Here, Edith."

She looked at the envelope. "Is this money?"

"What else do you need? Except a husband."

Edith looked at Joseph.

"He didn't say anything. I just know when you need money."

"I'll pay you back." Edith stuffed the money in her Hershey Kiss costume.

Edith rode to the Halloween party standing in the back of Joseph's truck, holding onto the cab lights, shivering.

Inside her friend's house, people walked around in masks. There was assorted conversation. Joanne, Edith's older sister, and her brother-in-law were there. Bill Lewis, her former husband, was there with another woman.

"I like your space suit," he said.

"It's a Hershey Kiss."

"Is that an invitation?"

"Why would I want to kiss my former husband?"

"Maybe I'm all you can get."

"I haven't had enough time yet."

Edith saw Charlie from the gas station. She handed him a few bills she owed for gas.

Edith listened to Bill play the guitar. Bix watched her watch Bill. Soon Bix stood by Edith. They were crowded together. Others were talking.

"I just got the idea for a house mask. Maybe I'm just glad to be out of that motel room. The front door is the mouth. The windows are eyes. The roof is the hair."

"No ears? Nose?" Bix asked. "I thought you already had a house mask."

Once Edith saw a bright blue ball fall out of the sky.

It was one of those things like Joseph's abduction. Nothing came of it.

But Joseph's disappearance had changed the family.

Edith was still haunted by the night Joseph had been with the unknown.

There was a brokenness she felt afterwards.

She was not able to get rid of it.

Maybe the ball of light had given her something.

How often did she paint her masks blue?

"I have a mask that's a floor plan. I'm talking about a house."

Other conversations covered theirs from time to time.

"A group of them militants live there."

"Send them to Bosnia."

"Except now it's Kosovo."

"Soon it will be someplace else."

"You mean the U.S. government—?"

"Would there be room behind the mask for anyone else but you?" Edith asked Bill as he passed her after playing the guitar.

"You finally got a job making masks—to the amazement of us all," he said.

"I like your mask," Edith said, looking at the Zorro face Bill wore. "But then you were a mask of a husband."

"You were a mask of a woman with a mask," Bill answered.

"We're saying the same thing," Edith told him.

"We aren't saying anything," he said and returned to the woman he was with.

"Why are you set on masks?" Bix asked.

"We weren't talking about masks," Edith answered.

A woman named Laura saw Edith and eased her way through the crowded room. "Edith—I saw a puppet theater in Tulsa. You would have liked it."

"I make masks, not puppets—and I don't like words." Edith turned her back on the woman.

"You're going to be short of friends," Bix told her.

"Just because Laura works for you, I don't have to agree ."

"What's the matter?" Bix looked at Edith.

"I don't like to be singled out," she said.

"You want to be noticed more than anyone I know," Bix answered. "Have you had a hard week?"

"I was nearly invisible." Edith walked off and stood around

talking to people in various costumes. She saw her sister again. Soon Bix joined her.

"If I could just make masks and not have to travel—"

"It's not something that would sell every day."

"I would buy them—Masks by Edith Lewis. Masks by Edith L. Edith McKennah Lewis. EML."

"The problem with that costume is that you can't dance," Bix said. "I can't get close to you."

Edith heard her name; she heard everyone clapping, looking at her. She heard her name called again. Bix pushed her forward. What was happening? She hadn't been paying attention. Edith Lewis, the Hershey Kiss, had won the costume prize without a mask. Everyone still clapped for her. She was surrounded by masks; Halloween masks, machine-made, but they were still masks. She was in Pawnee. She was not on the road in a motel room barer than the land itself. Bill Lewis, her former husband, was playing his guitar for her: the "Tennessee Waltz," though she was in Oklahoma. It had been the song her father whistled sometimes. She saw her sister wipe her eyes. What was she supposed to do? She stood in the middle of the room. She waltzed by herself. She held her arms out as though she danced with an invisible partner who could dance with a Hershey Kiss. She was in a friend's house surrounded by people who were friends. She was not sitting by herself on Mount Scott in the dark. The hardship of her job, the weariness of travel, and the worry over leaving the boys alone when she traveled were pushed aside by the Halloween party. Masks floated before her, none of them handmade, none of them she had made, none of them what they could be, what she could have made them. She was waltzing by herself to her former husband's guitar with one more day between her and the students at Eisenhower High School and the teachers who ignored her, who didn't understand what she did. The four more weeks of it lined up in her notebook, then the other weeks at other schools for the rest of the school year: where she had to go, and when, and what she planned to do. It all waltzed with her.

Edith was on her own. She had work at schools to last her through the school year. She had A JOB MAKING MASKS! What was wrong? She felt her tears. She stopped the waltzing. Bill had led her on too far. But what had he ever done? She hurried to the back of the room. She looked for Joanne, her sister, and her brother-in-law, but they had gone. People still clapped for the waltz she had done by herself.

Bix dried her face with his handkerchief. She let him.

More than anything she wanted a mask. She had been caught without one. She wouldn't let that happen again. "I want to leave," she told Bix. "It's crowded."

Bix helped her take off the frame of the Hershey Kiss at the car. She felt chilly in the sleeveless dress she wore underneath.

They drove to Edith's house in silence. They walked to her door.

"I'll pick you up for church tomorrow," he said.

"I don't want to go to Sunday school—just church. I have to get ready to leave."

Bix tried to kiss her, but Edith turned away.

"I have more on my mind than you," she told him. "Joseph isn't home yet. No telling what he's doing. You don't have children."

"Maybelle is sleeping on your couch." They could see her through the window. "If Joseph was in trouble, she'd be awake."

"You don't have your other brother-in-law in Texas; your sister on the phone about him. How'd you get your hardware store? How does anyone who is Indian, or part Indian, have anything?"

"My father married a white woman—she saw all the junk my father had. She had an idea to sell it—go into business—she kept books. I thought you knew the story."

"I do. I just want to be reminded sometimes things pay off."

The Mask Maker

Edith had been sick when they stood at her bed in masks. Her mother and father. Her sisters. What had she had? Diphtheria? Whooping Cough? Her mother couldn't remember if she'd taken the girls for shots. It was one of those childhood diseases they weren't supposed to get anymore. Edith remembered their eyes above the masks, looking at her as if she were going to die. One of her sisters had asked if she was, and her mother hushed her. They had lines going from their ears. She couldn't tell them. It was something you couldn't say. Sickness was a place you stayed by yourself. They wouldn't know what they looked like. They wouldn't know there were strings holding them to one another. Even now, looking back, she couldn't remember if it were true or not. Had she seen them? The strings were not something you could hold in your hand. Your fingers would go right through them. They were made of light. Brown as an Oklahoma sky with a tornado in it. A tornado you thought maybe wanted to be lightning but had to be wind. Strings of wind thin as a dog's tail running from one parent to another, one sister to another. Edith had belonged to the sickness. There were other illnesses, but not like that one. Maybe the masks she made were from that sickness. Maybe the masks covered what she didn't want to remember.

She couldn't remember when she had made the first mask. There had been the one in school. First or second grade. The children made masks. The teacher made one. They hung them on a line. She had wanted to put her name on the teacher's mask. It was so lovely. How had the teacher made it? Why had the teacher put her mask on the line with the childrens' masks, comparing hers to theirs, knowing hers would outshine them? It was a lesson in something the children couldn't do—making a mask as lovely as the teacher's. It taught them failure. Was it just now Edith felt anger at that memory? Maybe the teacher hadn't intended to show she could make the better mask. But what else could the children think? It seemed to Edith the teacher held up something out of Edith's reach. Showed her authority. Maybe the teacher was just wanting acceptance from the children. Sure.

There had been masks on Halloween also. They came to her house and she saw them. Masks she couldn't have. Her mother wouldn't give her

Every time the bucks went clattering
Over Oklahoma,
A firecat bristled in the way.

Wherever they went,
They went clattering,
Until they swerved,
In a swift, circular line,
To the right,
Because of the firecat.

Or until they swerved,
In a swift, circular line,
To the left,
Because of the firecat.

The bucks clattered,
The firecat went leaping,
To the right, to the left,
And
Bristled in the way.

Later, the firecat closed his bright eyes
And slept.

WALLACE STEVENS,
"Earthy Anecdote," 1918

money for one of the masks she saw at Pawnee Hardware. She stood at the window. The cold wind on her knees. Her neck and ears. Is that when she got sick? That bitter Halloween she couldn't have a mask?

Years later, Edith Lewis worked with masks. The masks she made had strings on them. She supposed she could tie them together if she wished. Edith traveled to schools to show students how to make masks; she never took her good masks, the ones that would be better than theirs, showing them what she could do that they couldn't.

She also had Indian heritage. Maybe she just got asked to schools because she filled a quota.

But what did that heritage mean to her?

Land?

Where did Edith get the Stevens poem?

In high school English, of course, but where exactly?

She couldn't remember.

But it was something she held onto.

She carried the worn copy in her box of supplies.

The firecats were her masks.

The bucks were the ordinary stuff that went on and on.

The firecats slept, but only for awhile, they they jumped in again and stopped the ordinariness from which there was no excape.

Look at the way the word *And* had a line all to itself.

That's what Edith's masks were—

Her *And.*

The land was flat and covered with low brush. The land was fierce with heat and wind. It hurt her eyes to look at it. What could she say of the Great Plains through Oklahoma where she lived? It had holes for eyes, nose. Maybe it was the idea of land instead of the land itself.

Or had the firecats been something destructive within herself?

Maybe Edith was the firecat who subverted her own road.

The bucks were only trying to do their work of being bucks.

It was Edith that had the firecat in her.

Is that why Edith was STILL in school? There was something unresolved. She had hated school, yet there something about it—some paint not yet dry that stuck to her fingers.

Whatever they were, Edith still bristled.

It was that way with masks.
She never knew what was in them.
They were tricksters.
They were maps of the way things worked.

Church

In church, Edith heard the minister's version of the masks' story.

On the cross Jesus became evil so evil could be defeated. Once Jesus was evil, he could meet evil on its own terms. On the outskirts of hell, Jesus and evil had a fight. Jesus won. Evil walked into hell like a dog following its tail. Jesus returned to good.

Evil still tries to get back. Someday it will have the world to itself for one last time. Then Jesus will come back.

How could she cluck that one down? Edith thought between the boys in Pawnee's church: by deciding that *whosoever* wore a mask would rise into the universe and be saved.

Edith thought of Bill, her former husband, as she listened to the sermon. She could live in the brokenness with her two boys. Or she could marry again. Bix would be a husband who wouldn't leave her; whom she wouldn't leave. But she would always be on the road; her masks behind her in the backseat. Edith was close to herself behind her masks. She could look at the oncoming cars. She had formed a face, an eyebrow; she had formed an eye, a nose, a mouth; sometimes she had formed ears; she had formed a face as wind formed a rock formation.

Something came together behind a mask. It was the way Bix talked. She had two faces. Maybe that was what her work meant. Edith and something else. Maybe it was what Bix found in church. If Jesus came to her, he would have to come as a mask.

In church, Edith often heard the minister talk about Joseph and his brothers from the Bible.

Jacob, the father, loved Joseph more than his brothers. Jacob made Joseph a coat of many *pieces*. That's what the original word in the Bible said: pieces. Edith liked the word because she made her masks from pieces. Edith thought of different pieces she used in making masks. But when the brothers saw the coat, they hated Joseph.

Then Joseph had a dream. Joseph was binding sheaves in a field, and his sheaf stood upright and his brothers' sheaves bowed to his. When he told them his dream, his brothers hated him more. Again Joseph dreamed: the sun, moon, and eleven stars bowed to him. Even his father was angry. *What is this dream you have dreamed?*

Edith thought of her mother and father and her two sisters, Joanne and Judy. Had they betrayed her? Had they always looked at her from behind a mask? They didn't understand she was Queen of the Indians. They didn't understand why she wanted to make masks. Maybe Edith didn't either. But she had to make them.

"You could sell your masks in my hardware store," Bix had said. "You could go to the Mayfest in Tulsa and get a booth."

Maybelle

You see your daughter-in-law make masks. You tell her there were Medicine Masks for healing long ago. They came from the Holder of Heaven. At one time, there were Stone Giants on the land. Men were afraid of them because the giants hungered for their blood. The men thought the giants could not be conquered. But the giants had a flaw. They thought they had created themselves. They were like Lucifer and his angels thinking they could be God. The men prayed the Holder of Heaven would protect them from the giants, but their prayers were as hollow as talking in your own throat. The giants kept up their raids. Finally, the Holder of Heaven took the form of a Stone Giant and shook the earth. The giants saw they were not indestructible. They saw someone stronger than themselves. The Holder of Heaven destroyed the giants except for one, whose name was Genonsgwa, who then felt mercy for men. Once a hunter found the giant in the woods. The giant said, *Dream and you shall see faces. Some are monsters, some human, some animals. Carve their faces from basswood and you will know how disease is healed.*

In those days there were giants in the land.
Genesis 6:4

Residency

On Sunday afternoon, Edith loaded the car to return to Lawton for the second week. Christopher, the next-door dog, barked. Edith, carrying a box, jumped. The neighbor called, *Christopher!*

Bill, Edith's former husband, drove up. He looked at the masks in the backseat and shook his head. He looked at Edith. She wore his old leather World War II style fighter-bomber jacket with a fur collar that she'd bought for him at the army surplus in Pawnee.

"I left that for Joseph."

"It turned chilly. He lets me wear it."

"I'm going to take the boys to Maybelle's." Bill carried a box to the car for her.

"What is a marriage, anyway?" Edith asked, continuing the conversation from the Halloween party.

"If you want to hold onto it, you wear a mask. You look like something you're not," Bill answered.

"What it is you couldn't show me?"

Joseph followed his brothers to feed their father's flock in Sheechem.

"Behold, the dreamer comes," his brothers said when they saw him.

"Let's kill him and put him in a pit and say some animal ate him; then we'll see what becomes of his dreams."

But Reuben said, "Don't kill him."

When Joseph caught up with his brothers, they stripped him of his coat and put him in a pit.

When a company of Ishmaelites passed on their way to Gilead, Judah agreed, "What would it profit us to kill Joseph? Let's sell him."

When the next merchants passed, they pulled Joseph out of the pit and sold him for twenty pieces of silver: and the merchants brought Joseph down to Egypt.

Genesis 37:19—29

"I was interested in other things. Marriage got old. I felt closed in. Confined."

"Well?"

"We found we were different than we thought."

"We are different," Edith agreed. "Not you are different, Bill, but me. I couldn't tolerate what I was supposed to be to stay with you. I changed while I was married. I had to wear a mask you couldn't see."

"I had trouble with your baggage."

"Why'd we get married?" Edith asked.

"I loved you. Still do. But you couldn't wear the mask you did when I met you."

"When we were in school?" Edith asked. "You were disappointed because I got older? Changed? Isn't that supposed to happen?"

"Why are we still talking about this?"

"Because it's unfinished business. Our new face paint hasn't dried."

"Where're the boys?" Bill asked.

"Driving around in Joseph's truck. They'll be back. I've got to leave. It's getting dark sooner."

"You didn't look bad—dancing by yourself." ◣

As Edith drove through town, she slowed and looked at the hardware store. Inside, Laura and Bix were working. Edith shook her head.

She started west across Highway 64 which followed the railroad tracks for a while, with the sun in her face. "Balm of Gilead" was on the radio; then a Sunday night sermon from some Bible church: *God saw that every imagination of the thoughts of man's heart was only evil continually* (Genesis 6:5). *The imagination of man's heart is evil* (Genesis 8:21). *Have you seen what the ancients of the house of Israel do in the chamber of their imagination?*

(Ezekiel 8:12). The minister found only one place in the Bible where imagination was a strength. In I Chronicles 29:18, where King David used it for remembering God's blessings. *Keep this forever in the imagination of the thoughts of the hearts of the people.*

Could Edith be a Christian and a mask maker?

Could she be a Christian and divorced?

Ministers had often rankled her. When Bill Lewis was absorbed with his business losses, without having business, actually, a minister told her that her burdens were overwhelming to her husband. She shouldn't bother him with her feelings. They were not her husband's concerns. She should go to the Lord with them. True, she thought. But at the same time, a husband who thought only of himself was not a husband, it seemed to her. Maybe she shouldn't be burdened with Bill's need to have a wife to take care of him. Let him go to the Lord for sex and supper and picking up his hand-pressed jeans at the cleaners. If he couldn't understand the hurts and frustrations she carried, why did she have to understand his?

Edith stopped at a gas station near Oklahoma City. She filled her tank. A woman drove into the station. She was Indian also (a mix of Indian). She stood at the next pump. Each dollar plunked like a bass guitar.

"Going somewhere?" a man at the next pump asked.

"Yeah, I just don't know where."

"How does a woman get so alone?" The woman stood at another pump.

"It just happens that way," Edith answered.

They stood at a rack of pretzels, lighter fluid, condoms.

"Coffee? Stop and talk awhile?" the woman asked. "I been driving so long I've got to wake up."

"I know the way to Lawton. I guess I can drive after it gets dark. My father's always there for a rider anyway."

"$11.27," the clerk told Edith.

They parked in front of the cafe which was a stylized tee-pee. The cafe was decorated with teepee drawings and Indian kitsch. The waitress wore a headband.

"I outlived my parents. The family was small anyway. My children are on their own. My brother's in Tulsa, but he can't come and get her. Guess that's the way it's supposed to be. You traveling alone?"

She had made a teepee when she was in grade school. She had never lived in a teepee. What did she know about them? She opened up the paper teepee, cut two holes for her eyes, and made a mask.

"Is there another way to travel?"

A young man in the next booth was listening. "You need a rider?"

"I got riders."

The young man looked through the window at the masks in Edith's car. "Looks like the crew I work with."

"What kind of husband do you have?" The woman asked.

"Enough of a one."

"Is he Indian too?"

"Part—" Edith said.

"Mixed blood is hard to deal with. So's full-blood," the woman added.

"What tribe are you?" Edith asked.

"Cherokee."

"I thought so."

"And you?"

"Pawnee," Edith answered. "But it's been watered down."

"What do you do?" the woman asked.

"I teach, sort of. I work with masks."

"I'm on my way to my sister's. Gonna take Verna and the kids back with me. Put them in school in Missouri. Verna'll be crying when I get in. She's got three of them she can't handle. My husband will help."

"I make masks. Well, some of them are already made. They're in the trunk of my car and in the backseat. Indian masks. Homesteader masks. They catch on sometimes. Actually, I get the students to make the masks."

"We never did anything like that when I was in school. Maybe I would have liked it better."

"Sometimes I think, where's my husband? My children?" Edith said. "I know my mother-in-law is taking care of the boys. I liked my mother-in-law more than my husband. Still do. Masks can run anywhere, but thoughts got a track you got to follow."

"Don't be too sure," the woman said.

"Of course, I've got Bix, my friend."

"You got parents—sisters?"

"My parents are dead, but I have two sisters—one lives with her husband in Texas. The other's in Pawnee. I have a dog—the dog is actually my neighbor's. I have a cat I leave food for, but I don't see her often. The same with my sister and brother-in-law in Pawnee."

"I don't have animals. They hold you down. You worry if they got water in their bowl. You worry if they got food in their dish. If they're lonely."

"You make too much over animals," Edith said. "I have to be on the road. A traveling job; teaching. I make masks that light a dark corner. Everyone's got someplace that needs light. I just look like I can't do anything. I work with masks. A mask is a little round snowball. It's like I run my own business. The Arts Council calls me an independent contractor. It means they don't have any obligations except to pay a stipend—no benefits —and they don't have to pay the stipend until they feel like it."

The woman stared at Edith, then looked away as if overcome at the thought of the possibilities Edith had. "Where do you teach?"

"I'm an itinerant teacher. I go to places they've already got teachers. I teach about mask making. A mask can weigh a hundred pounds. They would weigh down the back of the car if I kept them in the trunk."

"Sounds like a sweet spelling bee."

"I don't spell anything," Edith told her. "I won't work with words."

"I travel on nothing, too," the woman said.

They sat together awhile longer. Reluctantly, Edith stood. "It's hard to leave—face the road alone."

"About that rider—" the young man asked again.

"I don't travel with anything I haven't made with my own hands."

Edith drove off. Folded the Oklahoma map as she drove. "I know the way to Lawton," she said to herself. "I'm not picking up J. McKennah either. But when did that ever make any difference?"

On Highway 44, after the first tollbooth, Edith stopped at an abandoned gas station. In the last light of the low sun, Edith saw her masks hanging in the backseat. For a moment, they looked ridiculous to her. What was she doing? Masks made from dreams. She picked up some found objects to use for her masks. Scraps of paper. A rusted nail. A soup can with a faded label.

She drove off into the dusk.

Dear Bill, Where are you when my terror passes? E. ◢

Students came into the art room who were having difficulty learning languages. The teachers had changed Edith's schedule without telling her. In the art room, Edith helped a German class make masks. Then the teacher had the students write a dialogue in German for the masks they made. The students worked while Edith stood in silence. They read their words in German as they held the masks before them in front of the class.

"Warum sind Schmutz scheusslich?"

"Ich glaube, dass miene barhery Kaput ist."

"Warum?"

Something like that.

The students laughed.

Edith didn't understand German. "What are you saying?" she asked.

What was it the minister said when Edith and Bill were close to divorce? She wouldn't be able to support herself.

"Stay married," he had said.

"Why is dirt ugly?" they answered.

"I believe my battery is broken."

"Why?"

"Die Welt ist voll von Fragen, beantwarten erwarten," another student said.

"My world is full of questions that need to be answered."

The students agreed.

"Beantarten die Fragen bithe?"

"Siete 183, 1, und E."

The students laughed again.

Their masks mattered less than the words. Edith stood to the side, watching the teacher take her place in the art room.

Edith wanted to work with masks, but she had no choice. "I don't work with stories for the masks," Edith told the teacher as the class left the room, "I just make masks." Edith was angry that the teachers changed her program. She liked the students, she thought, as she cleaned the tables before the next class. They had ideas for masks and wanted to work with them.

Next, Edith had a class of Cambodian refugees. They were not familiar with English. She had a birthday party. They made masks. The teacher had them write in English. In barely understandable phrases, one of them wrote, *You have birthday.*

You blow candle. Soon you grow man. Have party no more. Edith looked at the students. They told a story with a heart, more than the American students. But they had seen more; they were from the outside. Edith could recognize their longing.

The next class and the next made masks. Edith heard what they said with their masks. Where did they get those words? Where did they get the images they made on their masks?

Now, in the art room, there were some Indian students in the class.

"Where is the heart of a mask?" Edith asked them. "A mask covers rage. Our feelings are stored in masks. Let your feelings loose in your masks. Let your feelings war-paint your face. Your mask makes a face you see from. Maybe we live because of our masks."

The students worked with their masks. They pasted the found objects to their masks—the soup label for a forehead. The nail for a war stripe. In the background, they heard the howitzers from the army practice range. The windows rattled again.

"With a mask you are seen."

After classes, Edith went to the office. "Where's my check?"

"Your check comes from several sources," the clerk explained. "The school pays only a small part. We're waiting for the other parts."

"Where do they come from?"

"The Arts Council. Several councils. Sometimes the library. We go around asking for donations."

"I left your school last week and I haven't gotten paid yet. How do you think I put gas in my tank to get back here?"

"The Arts Council said you did this on the side."

"Yes, the side my income comes from. This is my source of income. How would you like to get paid whenever someone felt like it?"

Edith walked through the hall to the art room. She felt angry. She hit her masks. "Get back. All of you. Dependents. That's what you are. Can't you do anything?" She knocked one to the floor.

Principal Potifar appeared at the door. "Everything all right?"

"Yes—"

The principal left before Edith could speak to him. She looked at the empty door. "Wordless. I leave them wordless. Hollow as a carved-out pumpkin."

That night in the motel room, Edith called home.

"Benjamin—what're you doing? Where's Joe? Is he sharing his room with you? If he gets back before we hang up, call him to the phone. Is that Christopher I hear? There's no escape from that dog. Have you got the backdoor open? It's chilly, Ben. Close the door. The heat will come on. Are you done bricking that bare place under the tree? Have you seen the cat? I'm going to talk to Grandma this weekend about Joe getting in earlier. And where is she?"

Edith wanted to call Bill when she hung up. She sat a moment by the phone but decided not to call. She didn't want to pay the bill to argue with him on the phone. There'd been too many years of not communicating, or their communication spoke too loud.

She paced in the motel room with its one lamp and a hole in the plaster of the wall. A bed with a sagging mattress. A veneer chest of drawers. Her house in Pawnee was filled with masks. It was hard to stay in the plain room. She felt the hollowness she had spent years making masks to cover. She imagined the hole as a small mask. The mouth of the wall.

At night, when Edith slept, the masks sat with her.

"You thought we were subject to you. You thought we were your subjects. But we have a journey of our own. We go to school. The students speak through us. We are words buried under slaps and hurts and isolation and abuse. We are the four directions of a child." ◣

"My daughter told me about the mask she made with my order slip," the waitress told Edith the next morning at the cafe.

"Did you see it?"

"Her teacher wouldn't let her bring it home."

"Why?"

Joseph was in high gear. He was like his father.

On their honeymoon, Bill was arrested for speeding. She sat in the car, sweating.

The sun came in her window; there was no escape from it.

Her cheek and right arm burned.

"She thought the parents might not understand."

"Understand what?"

"The masks."

"What's there to understand, Mildred?"

"I don't know. Why they're making them, I guess."

Edith crossed the street to the motel. She loaded her masks into the backseat. She had trouble starting her car, but soon it bolted down the street.

In the art room, Edith had difficulty getting the students to work.

"My mother works in the cafe," a girl told her. "She talks to you—"

The teacher in the room with Edith watched her above the papers she was grading. Edith looked at the teacher. After class, she confronted the teacher about not letting the students take their masks home.

"Why do you keep the masks at the school?"

"That's where they belong."

"Will the students get to take them home?"

"If they want to—"

"What will happen to them otherwise?"

"We don't have art here anymore. They may get thrown away. Can't you tell this room is abandoned?"

There was the crack that let her anger through when she wanted to hide it.

"You don't understand what the masks mean."

"You don't understand we're on a tight budget. We teach only what's practical—"

A new teacher intervened. She pulled Edith to the hall.

"I don't get paid. No one listens," Edith told her.

"Stay with me. I have a room. You can save the motel bill."

"Nothing I do words," Edith said. "Works," she corrected.

◤

Edith sat in the new teacher's kitchen.

"Why am I here if there's no interest in art?" Edith asked as the two women ate supper.

"We're in trouble," Luz said. "Discipline. Lack of interest in school. Learning problems. Emotional problems. Refugees. You've had them in your classes. They've seen family members killed. They've been told to go back where they came from, but they can't. There's disruption in the school. Unrest. The administration is trying everything it can. The teachers are defensive. They feel threatened. We're using several artists from the Arts Council to work with the students. Just keep making your masks. The students are listening."

"A neighbor had a relative who lived with them," Edith said. "A cousin? Nephew? I stood at the sink while he shaved. On his birthday, I gave him a quarter. My father said, *don't give a man that,* and I felt shamed. But when the man married and had a daughter, he named her Edith. She was killed in a car accident, which her parents survived. Later they had other children, but they were sons. I think of little Edith in a baby mask. I made a mask for her. I keep it near the ceiling in my workroom. I remember the man's whisker stubbles in the shaving soap in the sink as if they were gnats in the white cloud of a morning. The suspenders hanging from his pants. I remember how I felt about an older man. I remember the love for something I would never have." ◣

The next morning, Edith could not get her car started. She rode to school with Luz.

"I'll call Ed in car mechanics. He'll send out his boys to look at your car. They may tow it—I take my car into the high-school garage all the time—no charge. They need cars to work on. Many of the boys don't have fathers. Ed is a father mask for them."

Edith sat in the art room at school wearing a mask, eating a sack of Hershey Kisses.

"Do you eat every one you unwrap?" a girl asked.

"This mask is made from all the stuff left over from eating kisses. The little wads of tinfoil, the thin paper strips; the strips that are slightly waxy, the way you imagine the tongue of an angel. But what can a mask say with its empty head?"

"There's no head to a mask," the girl told Edith. "No brain, I mean."

"Don't be too sure."

Edith made a mask of Hershey tinfoil and paper strips, or *pulls*.

In another class, Edith looked out the window and saw her car being towed into the high school garage. Edith saw a horse mask on the line of masks in the art room. She took it to her desk and some words came to her. She got out her notebook and wrote them down.

Edith looked at the students' work, helping them finish their masks.

Finally, she held the horse mask to her face and read what she had written.

Edith finished reading in front of the class and put the horse mask back on the line of masks in the art room.

The boys in auto mechanics drive my car into the garage.

They lift its hood.

Now this is my beloved car, I tell them.

It has over 107,000 miles and I have driven every one.

It has gotten me back to Pawnee when I didn't have money.

It has driven through blizzards and rainstorms without quitting.

On those back-road curves where pavement ripples, it does not slide from its side of the road.

You treat it well.

Its hood open as a mouth, its four hooves holding still.

Pawnee

On the road, at the end of the week, Edith ate rice and corn bread in Spurvey's Cafe without saying anything to anyone.

On the highway again, Edith passed a prairie fire after dark. She saw the red strings of fire across the hills. Like the red wires in a toaster.

In Pawnee, Edith carried her bag, the boxes and masks, into the house. The dog, Christopher, barked.

Bix drove up in his truck. They sat by the kitchen window without speaking for awhile. The cat rubbed against their chairs. Finally she jumped on Edith's lap.

Edith liked these times with Bix. He could be quiet until she had something to say. She wished sometimes he would begin; he would give direction. Bill Lewis had always led, but it wasn't in a way that included her and the boys. They could come; he wanted them to believe in what he was doing, but it didn't really matter to him either way. He was going to do what he wanted.

"Have you got a toaster, Bix? I want to work on a mask with toaster wires for whiskers."

"You want wires from inside a toaster?"

"I need some red whiskers for a mask."

"They won't be red unless they're plugged in—unless they stay inside the toaster."

"I'll paint them red."

If there was anything in Pawnee, there were churches.

Edith had gone to one church as a child.

She went to another in high school with her friends.

She went to another when she married.

But she left that church after the divorce from Bill Lewis.

She wasn't going to any church where Bill went,

not that he went that often.

Hardly at all.

Now she attended a church with Bix.

But there were times she went to no church at all.

"You want me to tear up a new toaster?"

"You don't have a used one?"

"How long's it been since the one in your kitchen worked?"

"A year or two."

"Why don't you use it?" Bix asked.

"I keep hoping it will work," Edith answered.

"I inherited an attic, basement, and garage full of stuff. You could look through what I've got."

"What does it feel like to inherit anything?"

"I saw your bills when I brought in your mail. Your light bill's got a red stripe on it. What do you say I loan you money?"

"Whad you say you don't look at my mail?"

"You asked me to look in on the cat. You gave me a key."

"The boys can't be trusted to come over when they stay at Maybelle's. Other cats come in her cat door and eat her food."

"I'll take that tree out for you."

"No," Edith said.

"It'll fall on your house in a storm. You don't want to lose your masks."

"I can't afford to have the tree cut down."

"I got my chain saw at the store. I wouldn't charge," Bix told her.

"Then I'd owe you."

"Why you being difficult?" He asked.

"I'm tired. I'm angry at the schools that don't pay me when they should."

"You're angry at your husband, who left you."

"How do you know I didn't leave him?" Edith questioned.

"I heard it was a little of both."

"Who've you been talking to?"

"Maybelle," he confided.

"Where'd you run into my former mother-in-law?"

"Ben needed a ride to her house. I took him. She asked me to stay for supper."

"Was Benjamin stranded again? Bill didn't pick him up?"

"I think you're still in love with him."

Bix handed Edith some money. "You need to be by yourself sometimes. Stay in the motel this week. Work on your own masks after school. Nothing brings you back like working on a mask."

Edith accepted the money. "I'll pay the boys for their brick work."

"I'll pay them," Bix said.

Mask Attack

As Edith listened to the minister, she remembered she had thought church didn't mean anything. But it did. When her son, Joseph, was kidnaped, the minister read in Genesis where Joseph was reunited with his family. It was in the Bible, the minister had said. Joseph would be returned.

Bill Lewis had torn up the school looking for Joseph. HE GOT ON THE BUS! (the teacher yelled, terrified of Bill's anger.) HE GOT OFF AT THE WRONG STOP. The teacher and principal tried to hold Bill, but he was ripping the school, he was ripping his own helplessness. HE'S SIX (Bill yelled). The bus driver said Joseph got off at the corner WHERE HE ALWAYS DID! The principal said (the police said), BILL, SETTLE DOWN! The apocalyptic ride of horses through the air. How different to the parents (that event). The horses weren't there, Edith knew. But it was as if they were.

> Joseph's brothers stained his coat with goat's blood and brought it to their father. And Jacob mourned for his son many days.
>
> *Genesis 37:31–34*

Then back to her own needs: WORK! Every year the Arts Council said it might be the last year for the visiting artist program. There weren't funds for the program to continue. But every year Edith faced the teachers at the artist showcase. She wanted her masks recognized for that they were. But what were they? (They were her art, which no one knew.) Edith had to make them known. What did she do with masks? How did she do it? At the spring showcase every year (was it eight years now?), Edith talked about her masks. The teachers had to understand what she did. If they signed her up to visit their schools, she would have work through the next year again. If only to pay her bills. If only to make Bill not laugh (though he would).

Edith thought of reasons for making masks. She called her program, *Mask Attack* (with the subtitle, *I couldn't face without a mask*).

"What does that mean?" Benjamin had asked.

"Something will come."

"If the students could understand a mask," Edith said to the teachers at the showcase, "they could understand abstract thought. They could reason on different levels. They could understand something beneath another surface. Mask making is a tool transferable to other disciplines."

What was she saying? Edith thought. It didn't matter. They were buying it.

But in the end, she knew the faces under the mask of interest the teachers wore. *You give us time to grade papers. Make lesson plans. Keep the students occupied for a while.*

But she wanted to say that God Himself liked masks. He put Moses in a cleft of a rock and showed him a part of Himself. A metonymy. Isn't that what the English teacher called it? That's what masks were. A part somehow connected to the whole (all she could hold), though directly connected (a mask could be removed from a face).

Masks were horses of the apocalypse. Edith could go on. She could tell the teachers what would make them not sign her up to come to their school. She wanted to say she was working on a Jesus-in-the-end-time mask. A white face with white wool for hair (she had stopped in an Oklahoma cotton field). Two candles behind the eyeholes. A pocket-knife blade for a mouth. Let them see that one. She might work on a mask with leprosy. All with Biblical undertones (overtones, actually). War. Disease. Famine. Death. (What else did the howitzers make her think of?) (In that place where the high schools were named after generals.) They held her life in their hands. What would she do without work? Why couldn't she scare them, too?

Maybelle

Because your daughter-in-law makes masks, you tell her the stories of masks. It makes you feel like a girl again, when you sat beside your father and the earth was magic. Trees could change shape. They could become other things. They could be the Stone Giants, who taught men how to make masks for healing ceremonies. You have memories; half-memories that are not themselves but a cave for memories of your father and the ones before him. The words are gone, but you see they are in the masks your daughter-in-law makes.

"We are as great as the Holder of Heaven. We created ourselves."

The Stone Giants

Residency

On Sunday afternoon, Edith left her house to drive from Pawnee for a third week in Lawton. She found the toaster wires Bix had left on the hood of her car.

Another plunk of the guitar into the gas tank.

Another blip of highway lines.

Edith drove west on Highway 64 from Pawnee. The car still ran a little rough. Did she see someone in a mask standing in the field she passed? No, she decided. Soon she heard "Balm of Gilead" on the radio. *A mask is a balm of Gilead, she said, to make the wounded whole.*

Back to gathering straw for the mortar. Back to the story getting ahead of itself.

Edith turned south on I-35. She drove the interstate with the other cars. *I stay in Oklahoma,* Edith thought, *but those cars go on to other places.*

Edith looked at the masks as they swayed on their string in the backseat. She remembered Bix's suggestion of selling masks in Tulsa. What a dreamer. Then she'd be like her former husband.

In the motel room in Lawton, Edith brushed the air over her head in diagonal directions.

Northwest.

Northeast.

Southeast.

Southwest.

Whatever is crooked.

Edith read the Gideon Bible in her room. "The harvest passed, the summer ended, and we are not saved. Was there no balm in Gilead? No physician there? Why was not health recovered?" Jeremiah 8:21–22.

Edith spoke to her masks. "I see the students wanting to say something. I want to show them how to talk with their masks without words. I see them struggle with who they are. Maybe it's because I struggle—stuck between two worlds—the white and the Indian. What do I have but the smell of paint and paste? Wet papier-mâché. It smells a little like chalk and glue. A little like plaster."

Edith sorted through some found objects. She held a twig

to a mask for a nose. She held the toaster wires to another mask for eyebrows.

In the night, Edith heard the growling world. It had a large, open mouth. The world was coming for her. It would hold her in its teeth. Drag her from the earth. Her boys with her. Edith woke up in a sweat. She remembered where she was. Lawton, Oklahoma, wasn't it? Yes. Edith knew she was with her masks. She knew the masks were breathing. She looked for them in the dark. But the room was quiet. The masks were holding their breath, but she knew they were there with her. They stood between her and her boys and the growling world. Edith remembered she had held her breath when her father came in late. Waiting to hear her mother's angry voice, then his. She felt the past like a dust cloud over her. Her eyes watered. She wiped her face and listened for her masks. When she heard them breathing again, she returned to a restless sleep. What were they arguing about? Was it someone in the next room, or her masks, or memories? The masks were made of the same paper. Why would they argue? Masks were healers. Even Maybelle told her that. They were hunters of images. They were protectors. They were fathers who were always there. They didn't fight. ◣

Was it raining? Edith woke and looked through the window. It was still dark. No. She thought maybe it was raining behind the masks. She liked the times she woke from sleep, when her thoughts weren't in order yet. When they weren't burdened with feelings she carried. With masks she could be a maker instead of a receiver of the past. She no longer reacted to what happened. She made her own happenings. Her own decisions. That was what the masks gave her, she thought, and slept again. ◣

Maybe she dreamed her family still stood by her bed.

The next day, Principal Potifar came into the art room before the students arrived. "And what if I wanted to make a mask?" he asked.

"I'd hand you a paper bag."

"What then?"

"It doesn't happen all at once. You'd have to attend classes. Think of a face for your mask. Call it from its hiding place with your paints."

"What kind of mask do you think I'd make?"

"One you think you should make. But you have to put that pattern aside. Work harder. What part of yourself do you want to hide? That's where you start a mask. Work with shape until you feel that alignment, until your mask lines up with something you feel. That's the way it starts to work. In the energy that gets trapped between the face and the mask it wears." ◥

In Dothan's Cafe, Edith talked to Mildred, the waitress, as she ate supper.

"I haven't seen you lately," Mildred said.

"I stayed with a teacher last week."

"I hadn't seen your car at the motel, but I knew you were still here. My girl said you were."

"How long have you worked in the cafe?" Edith asked.

"Ten years. If you count my whole life, I'd say most of it. My parents had a restaurant."

"Why don't you have your own restaurant?" Edith asked.

"I don't know. I never had the money to start one. I don't think I would even if I did. They had a restaurant that was also a store; souvenirs—" Mildred looked at her hands. "They're dry as a dishwasher's," she said.

"I used to be able to work in water and paint all day. Now I use rubber gloves."

"My fingers look like dust roads," Mildred said. ◥

The next morning, Edith entered Principal Potifar's office. "I've worked here two weeks. This is my third."

The office clerk ignored her.

"Is the principal in?"

"He left for a Board of Education meeting in Oklahoma City for two days."

In the art room, Edith sat at the table wearing a mask. She tried to write a Dear Bix postcard but couldn't.

The students entered. Edith worked with them. "It takes some plaster of paris, calcium sulfate, casts, molds, quick-setting paste with water."

Edith watched the students working. Asian American. European. Hispanic. Black. Native American. Edith made a note of it in her notebook.

When the masks were ready, Edith mixed the paints.

"Sometimes it just takes a few marks—"

The students continued to work. Edith made suggestions for the masks.

"What does your mask want to look like? Put your paints down like brick—one after another. Let me see a one-story mask." Edith walked to other students. She looked at one student's mask. The teacher nodded to him—he should read his words before the class. They had worked on dialogue for the masks they would make, the teacher told Edith. Edith watched him walk to the front of the room. She heard him read his words.

Edith felt a vision of the masks in an old world as she listened to the student. She watched the other students finishing their masks. She thought she heard cavalry cannons instead of howitzers from the Fort Sill military range.

Classes of students entered the art room, one after another. Edith continued to work with them.

"Sometimes you can talk for the masks," Luz, the new

teacher, said when her class was in the art room with Edith. "You can make your mask say whatever you want. When you finish, I want you to put on the masks you've made, get together two by two, and have your masks tell stories to one another."

The students looked at Edith to see if it was all right to do what the new teacher said.

"There's no right or wrong," Edith told them, though she felt angry.

"We'll work on the scripts for the masks in English class tomorrow," Luz said.

"I would leave them wordless," Edith told Luz after class. "I don't want the masks to be a vehicle for words. I am a mask maker, not a maker of masks for which words are written."

"I didn't know you felt that way."

"What if I came to your English class and made masks because your words weren't enough to say what you meant?"

"It could be interesting."

"You wouldn't like it," Edith said.

"You leave out stories when you leave out words."

"Words squirm around the truth," Edith told Luz. "Words divide the truth into subtruths or almost truths. I don't like words. I've heard them all my life. My father's words changed meaning—he could make them say whatever he wanted them to say. My husband—" Edith didn't finish her thought. "I don't want words. I remember reading to the boys when they were small. I was tired after a long day, or preoccupied—thinking about where my husband was, yet I read those words. They told a story different than I knew. Yet I had to read them as if they were true. Only masks tell the truth."

"I think you're overreacting."

"I don't think you know what it feels like to travel all the time—to be away from your house. To stay in motels."

"I told you you could stay with me," Luz said.

"It isn't the same as being in my own house."

"The teachers want to make words for the masks," Luz informed Edith.

"Make them, then. What difference does it make what I say? I'm just visiting. Just passing through."

"You're here to help us. We're not here to help you."

Edith returned to her motel room and called her sister in Pawnee. "Joanne. What are you doing?" Edith could use her week's salary on phone calls if she wasn't careful. Her sister had a cordless phone. She could stir supper and fold laundry and run errands if she had to, while Edith spilled out her frustrations to her sister. No telling what Joanne was doing as she listened.

"You don't have to travel," Joanne said.

"What could I do in Pawnee?"

"Why don't you do something different than make masks?"

Edith slammed down the phone on her sister. Joanne wouldn't mind. They had had a long relationship. Joanne knew Edith's anger. She may have been glad Edith called her. Joanne was a stable housewife and mother. Edith was comforted that someone from the same background had escaped the disruption Edith always knew.

There is nothing but uncaring coming from his words.

He cares about nothing but himself—his money—his.

He is a mother's husband.

He is a stepfather—no father at all.

There is no love towards him.

There is no trust towards him.

There is no caring.

The next day in the art room, Edith asked for volunteers to bring their masks to the front. No one volunteered.

"What do we do?" one student asked.

"You stand behind your mask. We look at it."

"Do you mind, Edith?" Luz asked in the afternoon. "We wrote dialogue for the masks in English."

The new teacher asked for students to give her their masks and the scripts they had written, which she read in front of the class without names. She pretended to have trouble reading one.

Who am I really?
A pair of common shoes walking
*   through the hallway?*
One of all the cornflowers in the field?

"Whoever belongs to this piece, come up here and stand behind me and tell me the words I can't make out."

The student came forward and stood behind the new teacher, in front of the class for the first time.

Another student read.

The new teacher said, "I have two scripts: *Who am I—*"

What am I really?
A greasy fry?
A hamburger?
All the coke I have ever drank?
An empty cup?

The two students came up and stood together and read their own work. Edith listened.

One girl finished, and the other read.

The students returned to their seats. ◢

Sometimes when she closed her eyes at night, Edith saw masks. They waited to come into her sleep. Where were the masks when she was awake? When she was in front of a class? Was she influencing them? Was she their dreams? Things were not as they were seen. What did they say to her sleep? Were they masks she would later make? Did they hunt her? To use her to bring them from the dark into light? Were they real and she was a mask? ◢

How was she in trouble?
She was snagged on her former husband.
She couldn't love Bix.
Or was it a quieter love?
A wordless love.
Different than the love she had for Bill?

"Someone has written a piece called *One braid shorter than the other*," Luz said in class the next day. "Would you come up and read the piece?"

My mother had a birthday party for my brother. When he leaned over to blow out his candles, his braids caught fire. My mother picked him up and ran to the faucet.

When he came back, one braid was shorter than the other.

When no one came, Edith took the piece and read it. As Edith read, the students smiled, turned to the Indian student who wrote it, and gave him an approving nod. He was a Kiowa, Edith guessed.

"How did you get to speak?" the student asked Edith after class.

"By doing it. Sometimes it's the hardest thing you learn to do."

"Why do you like masks?" he asked.

"To speak, I guess. Only I paint eyelashes instead of quotes," Edith said. "A mask shows you yourself. It gives light to the room."

"I think it looks darker when I hold it to my face."

In the next class, a teacher turned on a rattling space heater in the corner of the art room while Edith was talking, nearly drowning out her voice. The masks swirled like a tornado.

"I like cement before it sets up," another student said. "When you pat it with the trowel, one part jiggles another. It's all wet when it's first poured, but soon it's solid enough to hold you up."

Edith made a mask that was a bed. With a little headboard and footboard. Pillows for eyes.

That night as Edith ate at Dothan's Cafe, she thought of Bix. Sometimes he was called R&R. Once Laura, his clerk in Pawnee Hardware who ordered supplies, shifted columns in the catalog somehow. It was Bix who opened the boxes of snowblowers, ice choppers, snow shovels, and roof rakes. It was the roof rakes that people remembered. The thought of snow piled on a roof so high it needed to be pulled off with a rake on the end of a thirty-foot handle was a thought they needed in Pawnee. In summer, when temperatures were over a hundred for several weeks, Bix asked Laura if she minded if he put the roof rakes in the window of his hardware before he shipped them back. That was the difference between Bix and Bill Lewis. If it was Edith's mistake, Bill would have displayed the roof rakes without asking. Bix could act like the rakes were his mistake and joke about them, but Bix had the hardware behind him. Bill had nothing covering him.

"I passed your table several times," Mildred the waitress said. "You must be thinking about something."

Edith looked at her. "Someone," she said.

"But you were smiling," Mildred said, and Edith laughed.

"I noticed all the schools in Lawton are named after generals. Eisenhower. Patton. MacArthur."

"I guess they are," Mildred answered. "The army base. Don't you get tired of eating in cafes all the time?" she asked.

"I travel every week. I have to."

The cafe was busy. Mildred didn't have much time to talk. Edith finished her meal by herself. She saw a teacher from the school and her family. The teacher waved to her.

In her room, Edith called Joseph and Benjamin, then her young sister, Judy, who lived in Texas.

"Ben—you keeping up the leaf raking?"

When she hung up, she dialed again.

"Sis? How're you doing? Russell's fine? Have you looked—no—I'm on the road. Lawton. When?"

While they talked, the wind whirled the leaves outside. The masks listened. Soon, Edith hung up. She sat on the bed, looked at the ceiling, wrote a postcard, then read it.

"Dear Bill, Send money to General Delivery, Lawton, Oklahoma. Up there, the silver sequin of a plane. Love, Edith."

If only Bix was a man in a mask.

She looked through her bag. "How could I forget what I need?" she asked herself. "I don't have my hand cream. I don't have my little medicines. My aspirin and vitamin C. I'm used to my little delights."

Edith called Bix, but he didn't answer.

Edith called Bill. He answered on the first ring.

"You expecting somebody?"

"You never know."

"The boys are fine?"

"Yes." He was quiet, and Edith knew he was waiting.

"Maybelle has them at the house?" she asked.

"Edith."

"I just wanted to make sure." She hung up before they could start on one another. Let whomever he was waiting for be his next call. ◢

The next morning, Edith talked to a quiet student who seemed morose. "Your mask has no face."

"I don't know what to make."

"Who would you like to be?" Edith asked.

"No one."

"What does your father do?"

"He's a minister," the student said.

"Make a mask of God's face. Make a mask that shows the invisible heart beating."

Edith continued to work with the student.

"You can make a cast of your face. Or you can make a mask without a cast," she said.

"Without a cast," the quiet student said.

Edith watched him work; the silence of the student bothered her.

"You can talk for your mask."

"It's the way God's heart feels when it beats, because He loves the world and He suffers when we receive a beating. To receive a beating is to know God. To know what He feels like when He walks through the world. We can't see Him but He's here. It's just that this's not His world. It's Satan's world. But Satan doesn't look like Satan. He doesn't wear a name tag. He doesn't wear a T-shirt saying, *Satan*. Belonging to God feels like when you put a blanket over the card table and it becomes your house and your brother gets in there with Willis, his friend, and they pull down the quilt and scatter your house."

Edith made her own mask of God as she worked with the student.

"What is that?" the student asked.

"God—with toaster wires for antennas—so He can hear our voices. Suffering is a mystery. It shows us what we are without God."

"God is suffering. To know God is to know suffering," the student said.

"I think of God nailing Saturn to the sky, when I look at your mask."

"If the planet is nailed, how does it move?"

"It's the piece of board the planet's nailed to that moves."

"Are we—are you going to hang my mask in your car with your other masks? I see you drive up to school with them in your backseat."

"I should hang your mask up there with the American flag. A billet for a slave auction. A broken treaty." Edith looked at the row of masks in the art room. "But I'll hang it up there with the others like laundry on the line."

"Suffering is the result of our mistakes," the student said.

"God knew the mistakes would happen and sent His son to suffer most. God wants us to suffer because we're people. God knows we suffer—like we know the animals suffer—but we don't do anything about it."

"Masks are a matter of reconciliation," Edith said.

"They're a matter of walking where I don't want to," the student said.

"We can talk about ourselves when we wear a mask."

Later in the day, Edith sat by herself in the empty room writing a postcard. She read it while she wrote. "Bill, the sky is a blue flyswatter on the handle of the tree. Edith." She pushed the postcard aside with anger. "Help me get through this day." ◢

Her sisters, Joanne and Judy, were the first and the last.

Edith was the middle.

"Our sister makes masks," they said.

"We don't know what she's doing," they said when Edith made masks for a play in high school.

"What will they think of us?"

The mask maker's sisters, they called themselves.

Edith had wanted to go to college.

By then, she was married to Bill Lewis.

"You didn't want to go to school anyway," they said.

But she did.

On Friday afternoon, Edith left school. The boys in car mechanics saw her walk to her car. "Your car running?"

Edith nodded that it was.

"Here's a radiator cap for your horse mask." One of the boys tossed it to her.

Soon she was on her way back to Pawnee. It was a balmy day crossed with shadows of clouds and sun. Edith liked driving. It was an in-between place. Not here or there, but a place between worlds. She came together on the road. Edith remembered playing with her sisters on the Oklahoma prairie. They would take their dolls to the creek and wash their clothes in the shallow water. They would lay the clothes on the bank to dry in the hot summers. Sometimes they would have to hold the clothes down with small rocks.

There had been a bicycle she shared with her sisters with a wire basket in which the dolls rode. Joanne peddled; Judy rode on the back fender. Edith ran after them, calling for them to wait, the sisters disappearing into the bright sun.

What had Joseph thought on his way to Egypt, his head and mouth covered from the blowing sand? What had he thought in prison?

As she traveled north on I-35 and turned east on Highway 64 toward Pawnee, Edith thought about the bed they shared during storms. And the parents' arguments.

Pawnee

Christopher barked when Edith got out of her car. She jumped.

The neighbor called out, "Christopher. Don't scare Miz Lewis."

Christopher still barked.

"Now, Christopher," the neighbor said.

Edith saw that Bix had cut down the dead tree in the backyard. She was angry.

In her workroom, Edith made a mask for the stump. It was a teepee with eyes. She remembered the mask she'd made from a teepee in school years ago. She remembered how making something Indian that was not a part of what she knew had confused her. If Indian meant having a buffalo, a teepee and feather bonnet, and the Pawnees were Indian, and she was part Pawnee, why hadn't she seen them? Why hadn't her father worn them? Why did they live in a house? Was it that only the old Pawnees had them? No, that wasn't it either. The tribes were different; not all tribes had buffalo, but why did everyone think they did?

Christopher barked as Edith worked.

Then the phone rang. It was Bix.

"I don't like you cutting down the tree without my permission." Edith still worked on the mask as she talked. "I know you were trying to help—I'm working on a mask. I just got paint where I didn't want it. I'll talk to you later."

Edith carried the teepee mask to the kitchen. Water from the sink sprinkled it by accident. She wiped off the paint she didn't want; she looked at the teepee markings that were accented by the wetness. When the mask dried, she varnished it and the color deepened.

Christopher still barked occasionally.

Later that same night, Edith heard the squeaking of the weather vane. The barking dog. She moved the cat off her feet. She took a mask for the weather vane and placed an aluminum ladder beside the neighbor's one-story house and climbed to the flat roof holding an edge of the mask in her teeth. She tied the mask on the weather vane so it wouldn't turn. Over her, the night sky wore its mask of stars.

She climbed down the ladder. "You just want attention." She petted Christopher. ◢

Bix arrived the next morning. He looked at the teepee mask she had made for the stump of the tree. Looked at another mask with a nose like the butt of a shotgun. Bix and Edith sat at the head and foot of the table, facing one another. The cat sat by Bix's feet.

THE MASK MAKER

"I used to hunt with my father," Edith said. "I didn't do much hunting. I just walked with him. Sat with him mostly."

"You've got a lot of feeling, but not much restraint," Bix told her.

"What if I had a lot of restraint, but not much feeling."

Bix looked at her.

"You didn't wear a mask to the Halloween party," Edith said.

"That was a few weeks ago," he answered.

"Two weeks. It's still on my mind."

"Why didn't you tell me?" Bix asked.

"I don't know you that well," Edith said.

"We were in school together. We aren't strangers."

"You didn't talk to me in school," Edith remembered.

"Bill moved in on you. I stood back. I guess I'm that way."

"You never had to take a risk for anything. You've been secure since you were born. You're the only Indian I know who feels he has a place."

Edith had both elbows on the table, facing him in opposition. Bix hardly moved as they talked. "I have to wear a mask," she said. "I fight for where I am. I have to stand in front of the Arts Council and explain what I do. I have to go through review."

"Why do you wear a mask? What do they mean to you? Are you hiding?"

"No," she answered.

"Are you ugly?—no," he answered himself. "Are you shy?"

"Not really."

"Why do you have to be other than what you are?"

"When my mother died, I pretended I was in Mexico. I stood in the cemetery and the pine trees were matadors. When my father died, the pines were white igloos on a frozen tundra. I could feel nothing."

He leaned forward in his chair. "It was December and the snow had begun to fall—and they are fir trees and not pines."

"Were you there?"

"Yes," Bix said. "I was always there. I remember you at the winter dance."

In Mexico the stove was right on the street.
You told them what you wanted and they
fried it before your eyes.
Edith remembered the dusty street,
the squat stucco buildings,
masklike, one-story,
painted turquoise and red.

"You were there, too?" Edith asked again.

"I was with your sister."

"Joanne?"

"Judy."

"You let us both get away."

"I didn't think I could stop you from running."

"I want to face something without a mask. I want to stop pretending." She leaned back in her chair. "What am I afraid of? Life without a mask is too plain?"

"If you'd get a job you could pay your bills," Bix told her. "You could work at the hardware."

"I have a job. After Lawton, I go to Goshen, then Duncan, for the Arts Council. After that, I have to get out my notebook to find where I go."

"You're a mask," he said.

She got up, stood at the door. "You wear a mask. In Sunday school you teach you can't face God unless you're covered with the blood of Christ. A one-story God—Jesus is Lord. My masks are a way of praying. I have to travel across the state every week—I'm on my own without Bill."

"A mask can't replace God. Sometimes I think your masks are like gravestones," Bix commented. "What are you afraid of, Edith?" he asked.

"Being cold inside. I feel like a cemetery pine covered with snow. Have you ever thought how cold a tree must get?

I could have made you a mask for the Halloween party. You could have asked me."

"What would I have been?"

"I don't know. You think of something for once. I have to face a class every day and come up with something new. You sit in your store and talk with whoever comes in. I know pressure in front of those kids. I can lose them in a minute. Then I got a class full of chaos. And the teachers don't want me. And Principal Potifar steps in just as I'm having trouble." Edith paced the kitchen.

"What do you want me to do?" Bix asked. "Marry you so you won't have to work? Go to Lawton with you? Sit in the art room with you?" He pushed his chair from the table. "Sit down again," he said.

Edith sat in the chair. "Just stay here and take care of Laura, your clerk," she said.

"You're a frozen tundra." Bix sounded angry. "You act like you want the students to respond, but they pick up on you."

"What have you ever risked?"

"You want to work in the hardware? You want to come in out of the cold?"

"I was made for the COLD. I'm SNOW QUEEN of the Eskimos. My teeth are made of ice."

"You can't get anything out of the students because the door to your igloo is a block of ice. It has to be cut open."

"Well, bring your ice saw and see what you can do."

"What do you want?" Bix asked.

"I'm cold, Bix. I'm cold to the eardrums. I want a heart wrapped in something else than snow."

"We don't have snow," Bix said, "much of it."

"I want to start out across the road and never come back."

Bix tried to hold her hand, but she pulled it away.

"You always say you can't wait to get back to Pawnee." Bix

looked at Edith. "I remember putting bolts and nuts from my father's store in snowballs when it snowed once. I should have thrown them at Bill—as if I could keep him away from you."

"What if the masks are more real than I am?" Edith asked. "What if I am only the head they wear? What if I am the mask? You've always known what's real. It's your Pawnee Hardware Store. You didn't even call it Bixell's. How imaginative is that?"

"I wanted to call it Gilead's (where there's a balm for everything)."

"You're getting ready to teach your Sunday school tomorrow?" Edith asked.

"This's the Bible Belt—my family's always been Christians. Yours too."

"Not as much as yours," Edith said.

"I had both your boys until Joe stopped coming. Then Ben followed."

"I know. They talk about you. They like you."

"I'm there every Sunday."

Edith got up from the table, paced. "You're at the hardware every night."

Bix looked at her.

"I called your house last week and you didn't answer," she said.

"You called me?"

"I thought maybe you'd remarried."

"I haven't been a widower that long," Bix told her. "Sometimes I'm afraid I'm not ready. My wife died the same time as your father. It was only half a year apart."

"The earth is a womb where we get ready for someplace else," Edith said. "We're in a world that is already gone." Edith sat at the opposite end of the table again.

Bix stood. "I have to get to the hardware—"

Edith followed Bix to the door and watched him back out the drive.

After Bix left, Edith sat on the living-room sofa by herself. She looked at the masks that surrounded her. Soon Maybelle arrived with Joseph and Benjamin. Edith hugged them all.

"The mail came, Mom," Joseph told her. "You're always looking at the box."

"Maybe your check—" Maybelle said.

"Yes—everybody's rushing to pay the masked lady."

"You know the story of the Great Spirit, don't you Joseph?" Maybelle said. "First he made masks—then he had to make the people to wear them."

Edith opened the front door and looked in her mailbox. There was a letter postmarked Texas from her sister, Judy. She read it quickly. She looked through the rest of the mail. "A letter from the Lawton School District." She opened it, grimaced. Your residency is cut short because of budgeting. Enclosed is a check for the first week you were in Lawton. Edith read the rest of the letter—the check for the second week will come shortly. And for the third week after that. She closed the letter, went in the kitchen. "What do masks mean in the face of cutbacks and diminishing returns? What does anything mean?"

"There'll be another school," Maybelle said. "Another workshop. Another library that needs masks." Maybelle left.

In Egypt, they sold Joseph to Potifar, an officer of Pharaoh's and captain of the guard.

Genesis 37:36

Through the window she could see, Joseph laying brick. Ben was swinging a bat, hitting a piece of brick. Edith ate a peanut-butter sandwich and drank some water. The cat sat on her lap. "Why're we left out of the world?" she said to her cat. "Nowhere to go. Nothing to do.

Nothing we can do. Everything moves in a different way than we do." She gave the cat a crumb. "It's economics more than spirit. We got our toes together. We get along better on our own. Sometimes I'm with people at school and I just want to come home to you." ◢

Edith worked on a scarecrow mask in her workroom that evening.

"We got to give Maybelle something for her trouble."

The cat sat by Edith. When the doorbell rang, the cat ran. It was Bix. Edith returned to her workroom. Bix saw the mask Edith was painting.

"I want a mask for my hardware store," Bix told Edith.

"How much do you pay?"

"I've already given you money. Make me a mask and you don't owe me anything."

"What kind of a mask do you want?"

Bix walked through the house looking at Edith's masks. Edith followed Bix. The cat followed Edith.

In Edith's dark orange bedroom, Bix saw a mask. "One like this—"

"You picked the one mask I didn't make. It's a Pawnee mask made of leather from an old saddle. The eyes are two buckskin balls filled with deer hair and tied with deer sinew. The nose is buckskin rolled up and tied in place, also with sinew. The mouth is braided with rawhide and corn husks for mouth and teeth."

"Where did it come from?"

"My mother had it in a trunk in the attic. It nearly dried out in the heat of all those Oklahoma summers. I oiled it, cleaned it. I keep it oiled. It's from a past that is gone. It's a tunnel through which the past comes. A way of life that folded. Had its eyes closed and ears shut and mouth stuffed with sacking."

Bix looked at a black-and-white photo of Edith as a girl on a pinto horse.

"My aunt's house—my uncle's horse."

"You said once you had an idea for a house mask. Was it at the Halloween party? I want the mask with ears, nose, and eyes, but no mouth."

Bix kissed Edith. ◢

Maybelle

You knew Joseph wouldn't come home. You knew it that day. You thought of going to school. Getting him out of the first grade. But something told you to stay at your house and pray to the Old Ones.

The Dreamer

Sometimes, in her dreams, Edith saw faces. Maybe they were the Old Beings left over from the Stone Giants. She tried to look at them, but they moved backward into her sleep. She dreamed of birds, of animals, of the land passing beneath her. Where was she? Why didn't she always know? Why did she want to know?

Even the wind had a face.

There always had been masks. They were a part of civilization. They had a history. Masks had transformed Edith. She could drive across the prairie because of masks. She could walk into classrooms because of masks. She could face her sense of loss, and anger over that loss, because of masks.

Once Benjamin carved holes in a piece of wood. Bill jerked it out of his hands. "One mask maker is enough." he said.

Sometimes she saw an abstract mask in her dream. An orange pear-half for one side of the face, a pink ball-half for the other; a silver belt across the eyes with two buckles for eyeholes.

Sometimes she saw an asymmetrical mask with mouth askew.

Then there was a mask with shutters that opened for eyeholes.

A duck mask, the bill made from wood from a dock covered with lichen and moss.

Edith tried to touch the masks as they came near. To see how they were made. To see what they were made of: wood, pigment, fiber, goatskin, wool, hair, teeth.

Sometimes the masks Edith saw were new masks:

An astronaut bubble.

A cold-weather mask, U.S. Air Force.

A respirator mask, U.S. Ohio Rubber Company.

And, of course, the baseball catcher's mask.

Sometimes a mask was sign language.

"I agree we need masks, but Christ is the mask I wear," Bix said.

Bill Lewis

Edith had seen Bill Lewis coming on the red dirt road. She heard the motor of the bike in the distance. It was distorted at first, as though nothing more than a fly buzzing the air around her. She was sitting by a bush mashing a hard berry, looking at the brightness it made on her finger, marking a rock with an eye, streaking it with an eyebrow. When Bill saw her, he stopped his bike and walked it backwards to her. He sat with her a while. When she started to get up, he drew her down across his leg and kissed her. Her hips were crosswise, at an angle on his leg; she felt awkward, off balance. There wasn't time to straighten. It was the unknown Bill Lewis pressed to her mouth. She straddled his leg until he let her go and she got up, her face red. She walked down the road, looking back at him once. He was watching her walk away, but he wasn't following. She tasted her mouth. Something was there that was not her. Yet somehow it was. Something had changed. In an instant. She understood a kiss. It was a small mask pressed to her mouth. She tasted her mouth again. A kiss had the taste of a mask.

"Bill Bixell's father owns Pawnee Hardware," J. McKennah told his three daughters at supper. Maybe he hoped one of them would marry Bill Bixell.

It was not a land for stories. It was a place for the sky to sit. Edith put her hand up to the sky. It was in her hands. She knew it was hers. It was her. The clear air around her was just an illusion. It was actually blue. It just seemed different from where she sat. Wasn't that what the minister said in church? All of heaven was hers? It just looked different from where she was.

She lived on the wide plains of north central Oklahoma,

where Indian tribes had been relocated, and buffalo had passed, and white settlers in their wagons had beat their horses during the land runs of 1889 and 1906, to reach a piece of land that they cleared of the few trees it had, and later the topsoil blew away.

Who needed stories anyway? Edith didn't want to hear anything about them. She looked at the land. She wanted it to be wordless. She wanted only the quiet sky over and around and above.

In church she sat behind Bill Bixell, but it was Bill Lewis she thought about. ◤

When Edith was in high school, there had been a dance. Bill Lewis asked her to go. Other girls wanted to go with him, but he had asked her. Her father, J. McKennah, was angry. She danced in the gymnasium decorated with crepe paper and a bluish light. Bill Bixell was there, too. Who had he been with? She remembered him looking at her. Once he asked her to dance and Bill Lewis didn't mind. He was waiting when she finished. Then Edith was with Bill Lewis again, circling the floor. He twirled her out and pulled her back. Later in the car, he told her he wanted his own business; they were still in high school, but already he was looking ahead. The night covered Edith with a mask. The plainness of the land disappeared. She had danced with Bill Lewis. Everyone saw it. She and Bill Lewis would make it out of Pawnee.

For awhile she was in the sky with the blue air. She had more than the dry, flat land. Now she had a husband and two small boys. She read to the boys, took them to their ball games when they were still small enough that the bats they used were flat as beaver tails. She looked at their arithmetic, took them to church. Maybelle Lewis, her mother-in-law, helped as Bill tried one thing after another and came home empty.

Monday

Bix was working at the hardware store, expanding it to the storefront next door. After school, Joseph and Benjamin helped him. Maybelle came with them. Edith and Laura washed the large plate-glass windows. Maybelle scraped off the paint of an old name with a razor blade.

Laura wiped the glass. "This is the third time I've washed these windows. I can still see the dirt."

"They're clean enough," Edith told her.

"Will you loan us some of your masks, Edith?" Laura asked. "The place is plain. Bix has wanted to sell your masks."

"He didn't tell me."

Bill came in the door of the hardware.

Edith frowned at her former husband. The boys were glad to see their father. Bill kissed his mother.

"I'm in a new business," Bill told her.

Edith looked at him.

"Satellite dishes." Bill returned the look.

"You're a satellite dish," Edith said.

"Mom—" Joseph warned.

"She can say what she wants, Joe—she just wishes she was a mover too, bringing the outside world to Pawnee."

"You always brought something from someplace else—not looking at what you got right under your teeth."

"Listen to those words."

"I saw your spread in the *Pawnee Weekly*. Just like I saw your other spreads— storage buildings, roller blades, skateboards, guitars, used cars—any honky-tonk carnival rider you could get your hands on—sticky as caramel."

"It was your old man who was all over the place," Bill

returned. "Who but J. McKennah never finished a job unless the builder held a shotgun at his head? Who killed everybody's grass—left them with a yard full of dirt and lime? I'm downsizing from my last business, Edith. Focusing—" Bill left.

Joseph and Benjamin frowned at Edith. Joseph left. Benjamin followed.

"Sometimes a man deserves what he gets—" Maybelle said to Edith, "but watch it in front of the boys." ◣

Edith continued to work on what she called her *apocalyptic masks* (leopard face, lion mouth, bear ears). Like the creeks she passed on her way west from Pawnee. Black Bear Creek. Lion Creek. Panther Creek. Benjamin watched her.

"You make masks for everyone else. Do you like your masks better than me?"

"No, Benj—I make my masks because of you. Sometimes I name them after you and your brother—Joseph and Benjamin. Jose and Benj. J & B. I remember looking at your little face when you were a boy—and making a mask from it."

"Which one is it?"

"I don't think I have it anymore. But you've always given me ideas—you're in many of the masks. Most of them. Sometimes people stay mad a long time, Benj— they say things they shouldn't." ◣

Then Edith worked on a house mask for Bix. It looked something like a blueprint: the forehead and eyes were the attic, the nose and cheeks the main floor, and the mouth and chin were the basement. Under the chin she wrote, *R&R.* ◣

Maybelle came over again. "I'm going to loan you more money."

"Why?"

"I lost a daughter."

"I don't want your generosity because of guilt."

"I don't have guilt about her."

"But you do about me," Edith said.

"Why?" Maybelle asked.

"You talk about my masks behind my back."

"I don't know what the boys have said—" Maybelle said.

"They haven't said anything —other than their friends laugh at my masks—"

"You have the house full of masks. What can you expect?"

"Can I expect you to understand? " Edith asked Maybelle, and saw she wasn't going to answer. "How did your daughter die?" Edith asked instead.

"Pneumonia," Maybelle said. "I told you that once."

Edith worked on a cat mask. Or a mask for her cat.

"What's your name?" Edith asked the mask.

"Jet Set. She jet. She set," she answer.

What cat thinking?

"Quatar," she say.

She Jet Set.

She set jet.

She set yet?

No, the cat had been nowhere.

Except in sleep.

Sometimes she quaked.

Her whiskers twitched a moment; sometimes it was a violent twitch as though facing headwinds. *Tornado-ish.*

"Maybe you should feel guilty."

"The guilt I have is for spoiling Bill. It doesn't have anything to do with you."

"Yes, it does. I was his wife. It gives you control over me and the boys. They come to you more than me."

"And that bothers you?"

"Here—I made a scarecrow for your garden next spring. We'll call it a sale."

The cat ran by the window.

"She always runs from the mailman," Maybelle said.

Edith went to the door and found a letter in the box. She opened it and read that the Lawton School District called her back. Money to pay her had come from somewhere.

Church

"Sleep with me," Potifar's wife said to Joseph.

But he refused (day after day),

When Joseph went into the house to do his work, Potifar's wife caught him by his garment, saying, *sleep with me,* but he pulled away.

When she saw he had left his garment in her hand, she reported, "He came to lie with me." They bound Joseph in Pharaoh's prison.

"Let's eat at Mae Lillie's for lunch," Bix said after church.

"I can't. I have to feed the boys. I have to get ready to leave again this afternoon."

"When do you sit down at the table with the boys?" he asked.

"When do you understand what I have to do?" Edith returned, getting into the car, looking out the window on her side as he drove her home.

Residency

On Sunday afternoon, Edith loaded her car for a fourth week in Lawton: her bag, boxes of supplies, her masks, which she hung on the rack in her backseat. Benjamin helped her.

Edith pumped gas. The mechanic watched her.

"Charlie, I got students who like to work with cars. Have you got any auto parts I could use for masks? Something small—"

Edith waited while Charlie brought her a box of used parts.

She stopped at the hardware with a mask, but Laura wasn't there. She gave the mask to Bix.

"Laura said you'd put a mask in your window."

"It's late for Halloween."

"Or maybe early." Edith started out the door.

"How much?" Bix asked.

"Five dollars."

"I'd say ten," he answered.

As Edith drove west through Pawnee, she counted out quarters for the turnpike tollgates so she could get back. Edith drove beside the railroad tracks across the prairie on Highway 64 toward I-35.

She listened to a guitar on the radio that played gospel. Then she heard, "Balm of Gilead." Those Sunday night church radio broadcasts. Her father, J. McKennah, thumb up, disappearing behind her as she passed.

For a moment, she thought she saw buffalo on the prairie.

◣

The next morning, Edith drove into the parking lot at Eisenhower High School in Lawton. The school was a long, three-story buff brick building surrounded by a football field, the garage, and parking lots. It was a bright, airy morning. The building seemed low against the Wichita Mountains in the distance.

In the art room, the students and the new teacher listened.

"The Greeks had masks," Edith said. "They also were in China, Japan, Burma, Ceylon, Tibet, Mexico, South America." ("The Greeks or the masks?" students asked.) ("The masks.") "There were (are) all kinds of masks: lions, bulls, monkeys, tigers, stags, yaks, wolves, dogs, bears, beavers, cranes, puffins, whales." The students looked at Edith. "Gorilla masks, antelope masks, elephant masks, longhorn masks, mudhead masks, war masks."

"Gas masks," she heard a student say.

"There were stone masks and wood masks with muzzles and beaks and trunks. There are brown paper-bag masks. There are masks with arrows of lightning and terraces of clouds."

The students worked on their masks.

"If I can't always drive the spirits away, I can fix them in their place," Edith said in the lunchroom.

"I wouldn't know you were Indian except for the things you say now and then," Luz said as they ate.

"It's the creative imagination that's Indian," Edith said. "Thoughts from the four directions. Besides, I'm a mixed-blood. I don't belong anywhere. It's the self I have to stay ahead of. How did you hear I was Indian?"

"They told us. We have to use—uh—"

"—somebody not white—and you decided to use an Indian to meet that requirement?"

Luz smiled and changed the subject. "What do you do when you're by yourself?"

"Cut newspaper into strips for my masks. I got a house to take care of. Well, it's a small house. I got two boys." Edith paused. "Sometimes I don't even know I'm Indian. I don't know the Indian in myself. My heritage is a mask I wear. Often I can't see what I'm like."

Later that afternoon, another class entered with two teachers Edith had not seen before. They shouted at the students. Bullied them. "QUIET! Make a MOVE and you're out of here."

"I've got a box of auto parts," Edith said. "I want you to pick out some things you want for your mask." Edith showed the students the masks she had brought with her. She showed them the masks that other students had made.

The two teachers walked through the students, poking them if they were not paying attention. Separating one student from another.

"Are there any questions?" Edith asked.

There were none.

"Make a mask you can't get off the ground," Edith said. "Make a mask you can't hold on your face."

"YOU WILL come up to this table one at a time," the teacher said. "YOU WILL chose what you want. YOU WILL go back to your desk. YOU WILL paste it on the masks you cut out. Ted—you first." The teachers pointed to the students one by one. The students took an object from the box without paying much attention. Edith walked through the students at their worktables. She didn't know what to say. She returned with the box of auto parts and handed more out to the students.

"Give them a name. *Auto head. Wheel face.* Now write something for them to say."

The students had difficulty responding. ◢

In Dothan's Cafe, Edith said, "Those teachers who came in with that class wouldn't hardly let them breathe. The pressure they put on the kids. I let the students go by themselves. Give them something they want to do. Give them ownership. They'll work on their own. Your children are all you've got."

"Sometimes you can't help but put a mask between you—" Mildred said.

A customer said, "We had one of those arts folks where I came from. He took a photograph of all of us in the town. We stood in the high-school football stadium."

"Where're you from?"

"Gotebo. Population 380."

"If I'm ever there, I'll make a mask for the town."

Another customer said, "They've probably been needing that for some time."

The waitress's daughter was behind the counter.

"That was the delinquent class. They're always in trouble."

The next day, in the library, Edith found a book on masks. One book had some contemporary masks (Indian faces made from hubcaps). She Xeroxed several pages of the book. The pages went by like highway stripes. ◥

In the art room, the delinquent class worked with their masks made from auto parts. Also their dialogue.

Edith handed them a ring or spark plug. She passed around the pictures of masks she had Xeroxed from the library book. The students seemed impressed.

Edith had one student cut pieces off an oilcan with a metal saw.

"It's easy to make an atom bomb," she heard a student say. "Getting the plutonium is the hard part."

"You can make a bomb with fertilizer and a yellow truck."

"Give your mask a name. His brains on fire. Dishearted. Blown to bits."

"Yellow Rider," one student said.

"Nearly Escaped," another student commented.

I want to speak about my uncle, he is a man of truth. He is my favorite relative, perhaps because we are so much alike. He is the one who built my car for me to drive when I was sixteen. He is the one who gives me courage in whatever I do.

Edith had the students work with short scripts. Then she called on a student to wear his mask and read his script. He didn't want to.

"YOU WILL read your script," a teacher yelled. "YOU WILL wear your mask. NOW!" ◥

The student walked forward. He read what he had written.

"Terrific," Edith said. "Now go back to your table—add some details. What kind of car? What can you add to your mask to make it say what you're saying with your words? In the meantime, call upon someone else you want to hear from."

The student looked at her.

"Who do you want to come up here next?" Edith asked.

He looked at the class. "Robert—"

"Show your feelings," Edith told Robert as he came to the front of the room. "Share your anger—your discouragement. It's a matter of willingness. You've got the whole world to talk about."

While Robert read his work and told about his mask, Edith thought of a car on the highway, the prairie full of masks.

The first student raised his hand. He came to the front of the room to read what he had written.

"That's it." Edith said. "Now work more with your mask. Make the eyes like headlights. The mouth like a grille."

She ran the class so that the students ran it by themselves—each presented a mask and story, then called on the next.

Principal Potifar walked by the art room, looked in disapprovingly at first, but stayed in the door awhile before he walked on. ◢

Edith and Luz worked with another one of her classes. "There is a quiet Indian student in class," the new teacher said.

"Autistic?"

I want to speak about my uncle, he is a man of truth. He is my favorite relative, perhaps because we are so much alike. He is the one who built my car for me to drive when I was sixteen. He is the one who gives me courage in whatever I do. It was a red '73 Volkswagon with black vinyl interior and now it's purple with graphics and has burgandy and black velour interior. It is going to be showed in a show this weekend.

"No, just frozen inside. His tongue is curled up like a rug. Choked up on the launch pad."

"Build a spaceship mask. Let it take you where you want to go. Make something that is just yours," Edith said to the student. "I remember when I was in school, I was supposed to make an announcement over the loudspeaker. I couldn't speak. The thought of the whole school listening to me wiped me out. Would you like to work with a mask?"

The student didn't answer. ◣

Edith and the new teacher ate at Dothan's Cafe that night.

"There was an argument at first over whether to separate Indian students from white, because it would make it easier for Indians to speak in class. But I insisted on leaving the classes integrated because that's the way the world is. I thought Oklahoma would be different when I came here."

"What'd you expect?" Edith asked.

"Wildlife, clear skies. I wanted to know how blueberries were picked," Luz said. "I want to make a mask for my mother. She died last winter. All she had was a death certificate. An obituary in the newspaper. She lived. She died. I think she would like a mask. I think I would. I could wear her mask and say things I never heard from her. When you come back next week, I'll make a mask."

"I go to Goshen next week," Edith told her.

"Next week is Thanksgiving," Luz told her.

"The week after that," Edith said.

"You have a five-week residency in Lawton," Luz reminded her.

"Eisenhower High School lost the week I didn't work. I've got a week in February—I don't know. Principal Potifar hasn't been—receptive. I feel like I'm wasting my time."

They finished their meal.

That night, Edith called home.

"Maybelle—you got Joe roped in for the night? The army surplus in Enid? Whad Ben want there?" She laughed. "Don't let him enlist before I get back."

Edith picked up the phone again and wanted to dial Bill, but she put it back down. ◥

The next day, Edith worked with the quiet Indian student. She showed him the picture of the hubcap mask.

"Put your feelings in the mask," Edith said. "It's always hard to talk—like when you come in out of the cold. I remember wanting—maybe I stood in front of the hardware store wanting a mask that I couldn't have because I didn't have a quarter or whatever it cost. Masks are a repair of those memories. You have stories without a mask to tie them to. Think of a mask that will look like the story you have to tell. Think of a landscape as you place your mask in a story."

The quiet Indian student listened.

"I like the oak trees in Pawnee where I live. They drop acorns all over the sidewalks that crunch under your feet. You have to duck under the trees to walk past them. I like the streets with names like Fourth and Fifth. The backyard fences and garages, the sheds and storage buildings, fishing boats and campers, trucks and cars with faded paint and rusted tops from the sun. Here's an acorn from Pawnee. Shiny as an eyeball of an angel. Here's another one, not ripe. You can have a green and a brown eye above the eyeholes in your mask—see the pupils on them?"

The quiet student worked with his mask. Edith opened jars of paints. Showed him how to mix them. How to place them on the mask. Edith cut the acorns in half. The student pasted them to his mask.

After class, Edith looked at the masks hanging on the line in the art room.

She saw the quiet Indian student had pulled off the acorns he had pasted to his mask, leaving two small holes. She saw he had added four feet, a head, and a short tail to his hubcap mask.

"—a turtle," Edith said to herself.

The next day, the quiet Indian student took his mask from the line. Edith showed him how to repair the small holes. She told him to finish his script.

When he was finished, she didn't read it but asked him to stand in front of the room with his turtle mask and read his script. "He called it, Turtle, because it was slow. *Move faster,* he said, but the turtle couldn't—it kicked—" The Indian student tried to read his script but couldn't. After an awkward silence, he tried again but faltered. "The turtle is the earth." In frustration, he choked up in front of the students. Edith looked at the new teacher, not knowing what to do. The boys laughed. The new teacher tried to quiet them, tried to protect the Indian student, making his shame worse. He didn't even run but cried openly in front of the class.

At the motel, Edith threw her things in her car.

She drove toward Pawnee beating the steering wheel as she drove.

Edith stopped once for gas and called Bix.

Edith drove to her house in Pawnee crying.

The masks.
The wind.
The road through the blue fireball
of the earth.

Balm of Gilead

Edith carried her bag into the house. Slung it across the room. She tore her masks from their rack in the backseat. Threw them across the red living room. "Traitors!" She kicked her box of art supplies across the floor with her foot.

Bix knocked on the door; the cat ran. Bix sat with Edith in her kitchen; the cat returned.

"I thought masks were my life, but they're nothing! That boy'll always remember— Why do I work with masks?" She kicked a mask on the floor.

"It's a part of growing up," Bix said.

"What would you know about shame? What would you know about having words packed in your head—until they'll never come out?"

"They do come out—in other ways than words. It will always hurt—that memory. But he'll recover."

"Just another hurt to carry—one caused by me—the masked woman. The one who comes to wound."

"I was teased by the other boys," Bix told her.

"Maybe I was tired of being mistaken for my sisters—but I always wanted a mask. I felt my naked face wasn't enough. If I burned with shame. If I cried. If I flinched with anger or fear. I knew every feeling SHOWED. I don't know where all the anger came from. My parents kept us together. I shared a room with my sisters. My father worked with his bricks. My mother made us chocolate pies."

"You won a prize without a mask."

Edith looked at Bix.

"Your Halloween costume didn't have a mask—it was your face I saw above the Hershey Kiss."

Edith got up, walked to the window. Bix followed. "You bricked half your backyard," he said.

"The boys did—I kept after them about it. I got tired of that bare place under the tree—so they *laid brick*. You paid them, didn't you?" Edith asked him. "You must have paid them well."

Bix stood at the window.

"My father's bricks—That's what I inherited—and a longing for masks," Edith said, sitting at the table. "But masks don't help. I thought they did, but I'm as empty behind a mask as I am in front of it. I go to my masks but nothing happens. I stay in prison like Joseph in your Bible story. That's what I see from my mask." Edith turned to the window where Bix stood. "You have your wagons, wheelbarrows, mowers, brooms, hammers, saws, nail bins, locks, paint and varnish—I have masks. I have time to think when I drive—Potifar's wife was direct. *Sleep with me*, she said. But why the desperation? Lust, surely. But there was something else—a hunger for goodness she saw in Joseph? The dignity? She recognized he was different than them—above them. It was the only way she knew to approach him. What else did she have to offer? I have been left out. Why am I faded, part-time Indian? Everything is gone but in the dreams." Edith paced. "I have a memory as a child. Wanting a china doll with a painted face I didn't get."

"Was the doll at the hardware, too?"

"You own what I couldn't have as a child—not even a Halloween mask. No wonder I want to be with you."

"Is that the only reason?"

She ignored his question. "I want to cancel my residency at Goshen next week—go back to Lawton. I was supposed to have five weeks—"

"Next week is Thanksgiving, Edith. You don't go to Goshen until the week after next."

"That's right! I have another week without pay."

"Your student'll be all right. Leave it alone." Bix held Edith. "I have to get back to the hardware—"

"Can't you change those hands on your little cardboard clock—say you'll be back in another hour?"

"I'll be back this evening," Bix said, and left. ◣

Later in the day, Edith read the *Pawnee Weekly*. She saw an ad for the Pawnee Hardware Store. It included *A mask, $15.00, by Edith Lewis.*

Bill, her former husband, drove up. The bell rang. Edith opened the door. She saw a man with a brown sack over his head.

"Bix—" Edith said. She pulled the bag off and saw it was Bill, her former husband. "Bill—" Edith was surprised. "What are you doing here?"

Bill saw the masks Edith had thrown as he stepped past her into the living room. "Roughing up your masks?"

"The boys are at Maybelle's. What do you want?"

"I bought this house for you. I can come and see my investment—" Bill walked from the living room into the kitchen.

Edith followed. "It was a divorce settlement," she reminded him. "I pay taxes and insurance. I take care of the boys. This isn't your place. You can't drop by whenever you want."

"I'm paying for the house," Bill said.

"My name's on the deed," Edith returned.

Bill looked at the dark green of the kitchen. "I feel like Billy Goat Gruff is going to step out of the woodwork."

"Who's that?" Edith asked.

"I can't remember." Bill waved the thought away with his arm. "I see you bricked up the yard." Bill looked from the back door.

"I hired Joseph and Ben to do it," Edith told him. "My father was a bricklayer, you know. He may have done the brickwork for this house. I only bricked where the grass didn't grow."

"I see the tree's down."

"Bix cut it for me."

"What's that white thing?" Bill asked.

"A mask of a teepee I made for the stump."

Bill looked at it a moment. "I saw your *house mask* at the hardware—Joe could have cut the tree—I would have—"

"I didn't want Joseph loose with a power saw. It was a man's job. The tree needed to come down."

"If you'd give a man a chance."

"My mother-in-law takes care of my boys and pays my electric bill," Edith said. "Why am I dependent on her? You could help. If you weren't wagging it all over town."

Bill walked into the backyard, looked at the teepee mask. Edith stood impatiently at the door until he returned.

"What's that on your neighbor's roof?"

"A mask I made to keep the weather vane from squeaking," Edith said. "You're the first one who's noticed it."

"What is it?"

"A pumpkin mask I tried to make. It may have shriveled—"

"Maybe you know what you're doing," Bill relented. "I sold two satellite dishes this week," he said.

"You can buy me a car—"

"Your hardware man can do that. You'd see two *flat moons* if you drive down the first county road east of town. You always liked the sky. You also wanted what was out of reach. You ought to distribute your masks through a carnival supply."

Edith turned a page of the *Pawnee Weekly* as though not listening.

"Maybe I could take a mask—" Bill offered, "—sell it with my satellite dishes."

THE MASK MAKER

"It never worked between us. If I didn't say something, I got angry. But when I said something, it made no difference. Our marriage was another lesson in loving something I could never have."

"Maybe we all know that, Edith—"

"I remember what it was like, Bill. We were stuck, both looking the other way. For years, longing for the way out."

"I remember when you didn't say anything to me."

"I remember when you passed on the street. I was walking with the boys. You didn't even stop." Edith looked at Bill. "If you didn't have anything to do for an afternoon, you'd still leave."

"You coming to the program this weekend?"

"What program?"

"Nothing." Bill kissed her ear and left.

Edith crumpled the brown sack he'd had over his head. She crumpled the *Pawnee Weekly*. The cat jumped on her lap. She petted her.

After awhile, Maybelle arrived with the boys. Benjamin saw the mess. He saw his mother looking frumpy. "Mom, you're as much fun as Grandma dancing in the kitchen to her recorded dogs barking."

"Did you see your dad? He stopped by for you."

"We must have missed him—" Joseph started out the front door.

"Where are you going, Joe?"

"To see his girlfriend."

Joe glared at Benjamin. "I got practice."

"I never see you anymore," Edith told him. "You're always on your way out."

Joe slammed the door. She heard his truck start.

"What's up?" Edith asked.

"He's in a lot of things, Edith," Maybelle said.

"Is one of them trouble?"

"You always think the worst of us," Benjamin said.

"He's practicing powwow dancing," Maybelle told Edith.

"Joe?"

"I think Bix got him interested," Maybelle said.

"No, it was Mr. Hammonds at the Pawnee Agency," Benjamin told them.

"Bix took him to a practice when I was running Benjamin to the doctor. Joe's truck doesn't always run—"

"Ben?" Edith asked.

"I stepped on a nail behind Grandma's shed."

"I wanted to get him a tetanus shot," Maybelle said.

"And a couple of stitches," Benjamin added.

"Stitches?" Edith asked.

"The nail was in some boards and I jumped off the shed and the boards slipped and the nail went crossways in my foot," Benjamin said.

"Benjamin—you're making my stomach rise to my ears—"

Bix returned from his hardware store. He looked at Maybelle to see if she minded him at her daughter-in-law's. He decided she didn't.

Benjamin went out in the yard. Edith saw he was limping.

"You aren't making much headway in getting things put away—" Bix said.

"I let things go. I get one thing started. Another pushes itself in front of me before the other is completed. I'm working on several things at once. I'm not ever sure exactly where the progress is. Maybe I'll even get one or two things out of the way, but then new things appear. I'm always in the middle of everything, getting nowhere, seemingly nowhere. Just give me enough rope to hang myself."

"Or pull others out of the mud."

"I'm on my way home, Edith," Maybelle said. "You leave again Sunday?"

"The week's too short—because of Thanksgiving, Bix reminded me. But next Sunday I leave for Goshen. I don't want to miss what's there. The way what's there doesn't miss me." (Maybe problems go away if you leave them on the prairie a hundred years.) Edith looked through the window. "I got one boy I can't keep home; the other I can't get to leave. Ben's out there like a squirrel digging for a walnut as if it was truth. I could not be satisfied with a walnut."

Edith saw Bix pick up a mask off the floor.

"I know those stars are lights gone out years ago," she said. "I live in a world already passed. I look at the masks in my workroom to see myself as I was."

"Maybe the spirit world tries to get you to face yourself," Bix told her, "just as you try to get kids in the school to face themselves through their masks—"

Edith saw Maybelle starting to leave. "I thought you'd stay for supper, Maybelle."

Maybelle stood at the door. "If I fixed the supper? I'm going to stop at Speed's Farm for a turkey," she said as she left.

The phone rang. Edith answered it. "Principal Pofar? But three days—I don't know if—a week's pay for three days? Well—then yes, the weather looks good—I could—" Edith hung up.

"They're extending your residency?" Bix guessed.

"Three days—a short week—remember? I'm loading my camel—taking my balm and frankincense and myrrh down to Lawton again. If I can get there without hearing "Balm of Gilead" on the radio."

"I think you're being sold—"

"I'm also getting paid," Edith said. "On the road, I think of who I am and what I'm doing. Traveling is my balm."

"You're the Balm of Gilead, Edith."

"I thought I was a mask maker."

Benjamin passed through the room. "You're always on your way out, Mom."

"I won't be gone long this time—"

"I want to go to the army surplus," Benjamin said.

"I thought Grandma took you—"

"I wanna go again."

"Which one?"

"Enid—the only one worth anything."

"We'll go Friday after Thanksgiving, Ben."

"Someday you'll see me leave."

Edith hugged Ben before he left the room. "I'll be sorry when that happens."

Benjamin struggled away, though he had a slight smile he tried to suppress because Edith had tried to hug him too tightly again.

When Benjamin was in the other room, Edith said, "Where does he get this army stuff?"

"What'd Potifar say?" Bix asked.

"They want to work on masks for the next few days—I'm sure the new teacher is behind it."

"What if I wanted to work on masks?" Bix said. "What if I wanted to use them to teach Sunday school?"

"I'm hired through the Arts Council. You can contact them."

Maybelle

You watched Edith make masks. Through the years, she made them and made them. You saw your son grow irritated. What could she do with them? You knew someone who had a child in school. An artist came to play music for the students. You told your daughter-in-law about it. You got her the address of the State Arts Council. You told her to apply as artist-in-residence. When you heard your son belittle her efforts, you told her she could do it. You rode to Oklahoma City with her when she went for an interview. You sat on the steps of the State Offices with Joseph and Benjamin. Afterwards you took them to lunch.

Now you watch Edith travel to make her masks. You watch her travel and travel.

When she felt confident about her work, you saw her ask your son to step out of her life. You saw him with his hand on the door. You saw why she asked.

Residency

On Sunday evening, Christopher, the dog, barked.

At the gas station, Charlie asked if Edith wanted to pay later.

"No," she answered. "I'll pay now."

Edith drove toward I-35, where she turned south to Lawton for her fifth week, though it would be only a three-day week. She would stay with Luz.

"Will she come back for me?" Joseph had asked.

As she drove, she thought about students working with their masks.

When she arrived at Eisenhower High School in Lawton, one student painted over the dried paint that ran down from an eyebrow. Others were reconstructing their masks. Edith was making a mask using the postcards she had written. She was cutting out the words: *blue sky flying over; fly swatter; terror passes; General Delivery, Lawton, Oklahoma; the silver sequin of a plane*. She pasted them on the face of her mask with paper strips from Hershey Kisses.

My brother's braids.
He cares about himself.
A pair of common shoes.
What am I really?
All the coke I have ever drank.
Nyob zoo os?
Koj lub npe hu il cas?
I think of God nailing Saturn to the sky.
Warum?
God knows we suffer.
I want to speak about my uncle. He's the one who helps me out.

There was a collage of words as students spoke their own languages.

Edith helped the Indian student who had broken down in class. She covered his head with a brown paper bag from the photos she had Xeroxed. He stood in front of the room. "He called it *Turtle*, because it was slow. Move faster, he said, but the turtle couldn't—he kicked it, but the turtle wouldn't go. The turtle is the earth. It walks slow around the sky. The turtle walks where no one listens. The turtle says words no one hears."

Luz worked on a mask. "I'll say the things I never heard from her. *My mother says my eyes are blueberries*." ◢

Principal Potifar stood beside Edith.

"I do this because I remember school," Edith told him. "Nothing I ever heard sounded like who I was. My Indianness was never recognized. I remember teachers who said, *Let her sit in back of the class. Ignore her. Do not give her anything that will interest her. Let her learn that nothing she will ever do will matter. Let her wither. Let her disappear.* I learned to live without community," Edith told him. "But we're defined by others. The masks are the tribe I make."

Edith looked at all the masks the students had made: a mask marked *untitled*, a car mask, a God mask, a waitress mask, a mother mask, a bear mask—no, it's a *buffalo*, the student said, full of holes.

Edith packed her car after class and drove from Lawton— pages from a green order pad flying from her car.

Thanksgiving

Thanksgiving was a last-moment plan. Edith liked it that way. Joanne was with her husband's family every year. Judy stayed in Texas with her husband's family. Edith would eat with the boys and whoever else tagged along.

Maybelle arrived late Wednesday night with a thawed turkey wrapped in butcher paper marked *Speed's*. All Edith had to do was put it in the oven at 6:00 A.M. Joseph wanted to go to a girlfriend's house, but Edith insisted he stay home until they ate. Bill, their father, might come.

"Bix, too?" Benjamin asked.

"*R&R*," Joseph said.

"He might."

Why didn't Joanne invite them to eat with her family? Maybe she thought Edith's broken relationship with her husband might rub off on her. Joanne made Edith feel the fracture of her marriage. Joanne had stayed in hers.

Edith woke at six with the thought of the mask she would make. After she put the turkey in the oven, she worked on a turkey mask for the open hole of the turkey's neck. Where were all the turkey heads they removed from the turkeys? Edith imaged them lined up somewhere.

Outside, Christopher barked.

Edith also thought about her mother on Thanksgiving. How much work she had done preparing the meal. Edith's mother had lived on the margin of her life. Angry that her daughters were not dating the right boys, angry at her husband. They'd all amount to nothing. Now Edith worried about the girls Joseph dated. If she could call it dating. What did he do when he was gone? Would Benjamin follow? Edith saw Benjamin walk through the kitchen, his unlaced shoes dragging their striped shoestrings like coral snakes.

"Benjamin, you up early?" Edith said.

"Christopher woke me," Benjamin said, pouring himself a bowl of cereal. "You got the turkey in?" he asked.

"Yes," Edith said, cutting a piece of brown corduroy. "Does this look familiar?"

"No," he answered.

"It's an old pair of your trousers. Or what's left of them."

Gravity was the mask that held Edith to the earth. Otherwise she'd be covered with an avalanche from space. She thought of sweet potatoes, gravy, dressing, apple salad, and corn. She would have to get busy soon, but she stayed with her mask. Gravy. Gravity. How close those words were.

Edith made a corduroy face with eyes and beak. She saw that Benjamin was eating grapes at the table. He made a pile of the stems he pulled.

"They looked like a tiny pile of twigs," Edith told him. Maybe she could use them for eyebrows on a mask.

"Or brushes," Benjamin said.

No, she would use them for the turkey's wattle.

What if she cut loose from the continent of her masks? (The

globe of her masks?) She knew she couldn't. Masks were her native land. Hadn't her ancestors come from masks?

Bill arrived before noon with some rolls. Edith was cooking the sweet potatoes.

"You need a dining room," Bill said, looking at the crowded kitchen. "If J. McKennah was still alive you'd have one added on by now."

"She'd just fill it with masks," Joseph said, who had just gotten up.

"If you'd move some of those masks over, there'd be room," Benjamin said, trying to side with his father but not feeling comfortable about it.

They ate at the large kitchen table; the cat wrapping itself around Edith's leg as she ate. The masks were the gravity that held her in the house.

Bill left as soon as he'd eaten. Probably some woman was waiting somewhere. Bix drove up almost as soon as Bill had left. They must have passed on the road.

Well, put another bullet hole in another Chapel of Love.

Joseph yawned at the table as Maybelle served pumpkin pie.

"Out late last night, Joseph?" she asked.

Edith looked at Bix. "Have you eaten yet?"

"No," he said, putting a sack on the floor because there was no room on any counter.

"You could have come earlier. It's not like Bill and I are still married. You wouldn't have interfered."

"I went to the cemetery."

Edith fixed a plate of turkey for Bix.

"Have you asked the blessing?" he asked.

"No," Benjamin told him.

"We'll have prayer over our dessert and whipped cream," Maybelle said, and bowed her head.

Everyone waited until Bix realized he was supposed to ask the blessing.

"We're pilgrims and sojourners in another land," Bix prayed.

"I thought we were from *this* land," Benjamin said after the prayer. "My ancestors didn't cross the ocean on a boat."

"The Pawnees walked on foot to Indian Territory," Joseph said, "from somewhere around Nebraska."

Maybelle said, "Our ancestors are from this continent. We aren't from another land."

"But we are strangers in our own land. Removed and removed again," Joseph said.

Edith looked at him.

"Oklahoma history," Maybelle told her. "They take it in their senior year."

Edith knew the history of betrayal. Betrayal of herself by herself more than anyone.

"I meant, *as Christians* we are pilgrims," Bix explained.

"What's in the sack?" Benjamin asked him.

"I brought your mother a bag of small objects from my hardware for her masks," he said.

"Have you sold my mask yet?" Edith asked.

"I have some people looking at it."

Joseph left after the meal. Benjamin wanted to go with him, but Joseph wouldn't let him. Benjamin watched television for awhile then left for a friend's.

Why had they been poor?

Why hadn't they been able to afford a Halloween mask?

Maybe her father was just back from the service.

Maybe he was just learning about bricks.

"You seem more of a minister than the minsters I have known," Edith heard Maybelle say to Bix as they washed the dishes.

"I wanted to be a minister, " he said, "but it didn't work out."

"You have something you wanted but didn't get?" Edith asked.

Bix looked at her. "That makes you happy?"

"Just an interesting thought— you've been frustrated in some way."

"More times than you know." ◣

Joseph did not come home Thanksgiving night.

"Maybe an alien—"

"Benjamin!" Edith smacked. "You don't know when to quit!"

"I was thinking of buying your mask myself," Bix told Edith when she stopped by his hardware store on Friday. "I want it for my wife's grave. The flowers I left yesterday seemed out of place. The more I remember her, the more she seems like a mask." Bix looked at Edith. "Would you mind?"

"I could put a coat of shellac on it to protect against the weather," Edith answered.

Powwow

Joseph was gone when Edith got up on Saturday morning. Benjamin was on his way out the door. Edith saw Bill's truck in the drive.

"Where you going?"

"The Powwow," Benjamin answered.

"Powwow. What Powwow?"

"It's been advertised all over town."

"I didn't see it."

"You don't see anything, Mom." Benjamin banged the door.

Edith called Maybelle, but she wasn't home.

"What's up?" Edith called Bix.

"What do you mean?"

"Where's everybody?'

"At the Powwow, I suppose."

"Where's the Powwow?"

"At the agency," Bix told her.

"Why doesn't anyone tell me anything?"

"I thought we did."

"Can you go with me?"

"I have to keep the hardware open."

"Can't Laura run it?" Edith asked.

"The Saturday after Thanksgiving is one of my busiest days—True Value is running me out of business—I have to be at the store," Bix told her. "Otherwise I'd go. Joe is dancing."

"WHAT? Am I not his mother? And I DON'T KNOW!" Edith hung up and called Joanne.

"Can you go to the Powwow with me?"

"Bill will be there—and Maybelle," Joanne answered.

"You could do this for me."

"You've always asked me to do a lot."

"Joseph needs someone there."

Joanne said, "He has someone there. Edith—Bill has another woman. *They'll* be there."

"Bill has always had another woman," Edith said quickly, then asked, "How do you know?"

"Bill brought her to one of Benjamin's programs. I don't think it would mean anything to Joseph to see me there."

"You're his Aunt Joanne."

"I have my own family. How many places do you go to see my children?"

"I want someone to go with me. I'm on the road by myself all the time."

"You're going to have to go by yourself." ◣

Edith drove to the Pawnee Agency on the east side of Pawnee. It was an old brick building in a compound of brick buildings. She could hear the drumming from the parking lot.

Edith felt awkward as she found her way through the crowd. She found a seat in the bleachers. She watched the dancers. She saw Joseph.

She looked at the crowd. Where had everyone come from?

I go anywhere because of my blue face. As long as the sky is blue I am there.

The rows in front of Edith—were—what was it? Who? Bill and a woman. Beside him were Benjamin, a friend of Benjamin, and a girl. Maybe it was the girl Joseph had been dating. How could Bill bring another woman?

How long had he been bringing the woman to the boys' programs? Edith traveled through the week. She missed a lot of things the boys were doing. What was Bill thinking? And there was Maybelle sitting with them! TRAITOR, Edith wanted to yell.

After the round was over and Joseph left the floor, Edith left.

She went back to the house, threw a mask off the table, and sat with her head in her hands. She put another mask to her face. It was a dam. She took it off and the backed-up water flooded.

Was she the woman at the Halloween party? Edith couldn't remember. Was she the woman whose call Bill was waiting for when Edith had phoned him? Edith sensed he had been disappointed when he answered and heard her voice. Was she where Bill had gone so soon after Thanksgiving dinner? What was going on that Edith didn't know? She had to travel. It was her job. Where would she be without the road?

What did Bill do when she was gone? Had he brought the woman to Edith's house? Her house? Filled with masks. Had the woman seen them? Did she talk about the masks in Edith's house to others? Did she commiserate with Bill about the strange former wife he had? What did they do while she was gone? Were Bill and his girlfriend now parents to the boys? Why hadn't Benjamin told her?

She flung another mask across the room.

She cried the rest of the morning, the cat sitting on her feet.

In the afternoon, Edith heard Benjamin come in the front door. He was alone. They must have let him out at the door.

"Who was that woman?"

"Dad's girlfriend."

"What's her name?"

"Joel (Jo-elle)," Benjamin said.

"Where did he find her?"

"She lives here, Mom—in Pawnee."

That was it. She was younger than Bill. Somewhere back in school, there she'd been. The new mother of Edith's boys.

"Has he had her here?"

"Sometimes she's with him when he comes to pick me up."

"Does she come in the house?"

"No."

"Are you sure?"

"Once she came in the front door."

Edith screamed.

"She just stayed at the door. She didn't look around the house," Benjamin tried to tell her.

Edith called Bill. Somehow he answered.

"I don't want you to bring your women to my house!" Edith screamed.

"It's just one woman."

"Keep them away from my house and my boys!"

"They're my boys too, Edith. You can't tell me what to do."

Edith didn't give Bill a chance to say anything else. She was all the FURIES rolled into one woman. BETRAYED by her former husband. SPIED upon by a woman who had taken her boys. Even Maybelle was in on it!

Edith called Maybelle. "You too, Brutus. You didn't tell me Bill had a woman he brought around the boys."

"They've been going together for some time."

"You didn't tell me."

"I didn't want to listen to you yell."

"That's a poor excuse."

Benjamin must have gone somewhere. Edith couldn't find him when she got off the phone. Maybe he had fled because of her fury. She threw a shoe box full of paint against the fridge. It broke and splattered colors on the wall and floor.

Masks covered fury. Could they smother the full blaze of her rage? What had they done behind her back? Talked. Made fun. Child stuff. Didn't they know the whole world wore a mask? The universe was a mask. Look at it at night. A flecked face speckled with white dots. Nothing known. The mouth hole closed; the eyeholes blinking once in awhile. ◣

Growing up and leaving Edith in the dust is what had kidnapped Joseph.

Bix came to the house as soon as he closed the hardware store. He handed Edith fifteen dollars. "Your mask sold today."

"You bought it?" she asked.

"No, someone came in and wanted it."

"Who?"

"I don't know who they were," Bix said. "There are people around Pawnee I don't know."

"Why did they want it?"

"I didn't ask," Bix said. "I just told them it was made by a local artist."

"I'll make you another one for your wife," Edith said.

"My deceased wife," Bix reminded her. He asked Edith again if she minded.

"No," she answered. "There are other women intruding in my life." She looked at Bix.

He fingered the mess from Edith's mask making as he sat with her and her cat.

"I'll make another mask for your store."

"Where do you get the ideas for your masks?" Bix asked.

"They come through dreams. From the past. The land. Sometimes I pick them up as I drive." Edith paused. "Did you know about Joel too?"

"Who?"

"Jo-elle. The woman Bill is dating."

"Joel Thomas—I've seen them."

"You didn't tell me?" Edith said.

"You're divorced. Bill can do what he wants. It isn't like he's cheating."

"It is when he's around the boys."

"Come on, Edith. You wanted to get rid of him. Do you think he would live without a girlfriend?"

"He can have a girlfriend if he wants. Not around my house, though. Not around the boys."

"You're gone all the time," Bix said. "You should be happy he goes to the boys' programs since you can't."

"Well at least you say *can't* instead of *don't*," Edith responded. "Where did she come from?"

"We figured she's eight years younger than Bill."

"We?" Edith asked.

"Judy and I," Bix told her.

"You talked to Judy about this without telling me?"

"I just mentioned it to her on the phone."

"Judy's in Texas!" Edith exclaimed.

"I talk to her now and then," Bix said.

"Joanne too?"

"Yes."

"That makes me angry—angrier—" Edith said. "Not just about Bill—but about no one telling me."

"We didn't want to upset you. It's not that important, Edith."

"It is, because you kept it from me."

"We didn't want you thinking about it on the road."

"Would you stop saying WE! Everyone knew—" Edith cried. "I'm going to be thinking about the way you all handled it when I'm on the road."

"You could have been thinking about why Joseph was always with Bill."

"Why?" Edith asked.

"Bill's girlfriend is Joseph's girlfriend's aunt."

"Bill fixed his son up with his girlfriend's niece?" Edith was incredulous.

"Bill met her through Joseph's girlfriend."

"This is too much to hear all at once," Edith covered her ears.

"What do you think we do when you're gone? Stand frozen in place until you return, when we're allowed to move again?" Now Bix was angry. "We have our own lives, Edith. I can't take care of everything you think I should take care of for you. You don't have to be on the road all the time."

"You think I choose to be gone?" Edith asked

"It seems to me you could do something around here. Isn't there something in Pawnee?"

"I MAKE MASKS!" Edith said. "I have to travel."

"It seems to me you're still playing dolls."

The Maker

The masks they had worn when Edith was sick looked like igloos. A white cup across the nose and mouth. She could have been an Eskimo. She could have hunted polar bears. It was cold in Oklahoma at times. They had snow every year. Sometimes blizzards. The highway would be closed. Edith loved the high buzz of weather so white and cold it was blue. But more often, there would be an ice storm that broke tree limbs and pulled down electrical wires. How often she felt frozen. Bix had called her a tundra. Was that it? If only she would not turn cold. How often she felt like she spoke blubber.

Church

Pharaoh had a dream of seven fat cows and seven lean cows.

The butler said, "When I was in prison, there was a man who interpreted my dream."

Pharaoh sent for Joseph and Joseph told Pharaoh there would be seven years of plenty and seven years of famine.

Pharaoh made Joseph overseer of his storehouses.

"The story of Joseph was written after the fact," the minister said. "We don't know what Joseph thought in Canaan when his brothers took his coat. We don't know what Joseph thought in the pit where his brothers threw him. We don't know how he felt on his way from Canaan to Egypt. Or the two years he spent in prison when he had done nothing wrong. We read the story clean as a storehouse after a famine. Joseph knew betrayal. But we don't read how he felt."

After church, Edith heard Maybelle talking to Benjamin in the other room. "In 1806, Lewis and Clark returned from the headwaters of the Mis-souri with maps. They unfolded the maps and got down on the floor and showed Thomas

Look there—that Mandan village on the Missouri River in North Dakota—they would be dead of smallpox in a year.

Jefferson what he was president of. That's what the Oval Office is for. Can you imagine? The men kneeling over the hand-drawn maps, following the Missouri with their finger all the way back to the Pacific."

Edith worked with the thought of masks as a map, *one braid shorter than the other.* Edith worked with the thought of the mask of God. She thought of brick and mortar. She thought of the famine of art. ◣

Was he really a one-story God?

Maybe Edith was more of a one-story woman.

Edith's five weeks in Lawton were finished. Now she would be on her way to Goshen in the Oklahoma panhandle.

Bix had wanted her to go to a hardware convention in Tulsa. "We'd have separate rooms," he told her.

"But they wouldn't know that."

"They know me," he said.

"I don't want to go to a hardware convention. Take Laura."

"I probably will," Bix said. "I'll take Joseph and Benjamin if you want."

"Bill might want to go," Edith said. "Why don't you hire him?"

"I tried once. He wanted to work for himself."

"Don't I know." ◣

Edith thought of her father, who had come home gray and powdery from the mortar he used between the bricks, his dark skin tanned to horsehide under his ghostly apparition. His cap backwards, his sleeves cut out of his shirts. His three daughters waiting at the table, looking at him in awe. All of them, his country of worshipers. Maybe the masks Edith first made were of him. The J. McKennah somewhere under the cement dust. The gray powder that worked its way into his heart. Ghostly and dried out from too much sun. (Bricks were his masks.)

Joseph's brothers came from Canaan to Egypt to buy wheat during the famine. They didn't recognize Joseph. He made them go back for Jacob and Benjamin, their father and youngest brother. They all came to Egypt and were reunited.

History

Edith always heard the train going by. The railroad tracks were a part of Pawnee. Wasn't it the train trestle across Black Bear Creek where Bill had written Edith's name?

The large stone Pawnee County Courthouse sat on the mound of the town square. Around the square, on brick streets, were the old buildings: the 1906 Bruington Thompson Bldg, the 1911 Lundquist Bldg, the 1948 Ramey Bldg, the Lillie Bldg, the Pawnee Bank, Pawnee Bill's Trading Post, City Hall, CPA, Attorneys at Law, Roadrunner Hotel, Poteet Funeral.

Beyond the square were the County Fairgrounds and Memorial Field, the U.S. Department of the Interior, Bureau of

Indian Affairs, Pawnee Agency. Beyond that, to the east, the wooded hills of northeastern Oklahoma.

Edith remembered the red dirt roads, the russet trees, the bottles in the ditches along the roads where she rode with Bill. The dirt still pecking under the car when they got to the paved road.

Sometimes, when they passed the Pawnee Agency, she saw the hull of an old bus abandoned in a field. Edith remembered she had imagined traveling with her masks in that bus. Had she dreamed of masks even then? ◥

To the west of Pawnee on Highway 64, on Blue Hawk Peak, was Pawnee Bill's Museum and Ranch, which Edith passed each time she left town. Pawnee Bill was a white man who had come to Indian Territory in the land run of April 22, 1889.

William Cody, known as Buffalo Bill, asked Gordon William Lillie, Pawnee Bill, to join him touring with his Wild West Show. Pawnee Bill and Buffalo Bill went into business in 1908 as *Buffalo Bill's Wild West Show and Pawnee Bill's Far East Show.*

Edith had read about the show; how frontiersmen, Indians, cowboys, trappers, gauchos, Arabs, and even Cossacks had come whooping into the arena with *war cries surpassing in Truthfulness and Intensity anything before it.* The shows were the *Amusement Triumph of the Age.* The shows received a *standing ovation in every town.* The arena had seated ten thousand.

Pawnee Bill built his house (mansion) on the hill he purchased from Blue Hawk, a Pawnee medicine man, with the tour money Pawnee Bill and Buffalo Bill made before they went bust in 1913.

The house was on the National Register of Historical Places.

The rooms, painted dark red, mustard yellow, dark green, and dark turquoise, were the place where Edith had gotten the idea for the rooms in her house, Bix frowning as he mixed the paints for her at his hardware store. There also were dark mahogany wood paneling, which Edith couldn't afford, elaborate borders around the succulent rooms, various fireplaces, beveled glass.

Besides the house, on the grounds of the Pawnee Bill Ranch, were a museum, a barn, a log cabin where Pawnee Bill and his wife, May, lived before they went into show business, and a blacksmith's shop (a forerunner of the hardware).

Later, Pawnee Bill built an Old West Town east of Pawnee: *"Out Where the West Remains" Pawnee Bill's Old Town Indian Trading Post. Free Indian Museum. Boy Scout and Tourist Camp. Most novel attraction of Western Material ever assembled including: Genuine Stage Coaches. Buck Boards. Prairie Schooners. Indian Travoys. Indian Village of Chiefs. Squaws. Papooses and Braves. Gentle Indian and Shetland Ponies. Herds of American Buffalo. Texas Steers etc. etc.*

Did he ever stop?

Featuring a Mexican contra dance on horseback, a Mexican band of ten pieces, a cremation by the Mojave Indians, and Little Virginia Ellis, the "only survivor of the Mountain Meadows Massacre." Also featuring Arabian Acrobats, the Human Pin Cushion, the Fire King, a contortionist, an India rubber man, a snake charmer, a knife / battle ax fight, the Big-Footed Boy, the Spotted Sisters, performing Sioux, African and American songs, dance and other acrobatic feats.

The Old West Town burned in 1939.

Edith remembered the bits in the barn at the Pawnee Bill Ranch that turned the horses' mouths. That taught them to turn with an instrument of pain. Is that the way Edith learned? And what was it she had to learn?

Major Gordon William Lillie, Pawnee Bill, was a showman at heart.

That's what Bill Lewis was. A showman. He said his grand-father had been a sharpshooter and trick rider in the early shows.

Edith believed it.

She'd seen the photos of horses with angora saddlebags, braided horsehair headstalls, Texas stock saddles with silver stars on tapaderos; their riders in sheepskin chaps.

The Pawnee

In Pawnee Bill's museum, the buffalo head was cracking around the eyes. Edith thought of the people she was a part of, and not a part of, at the same time.

A monument on the Pawnee Agency read:

In 1875, the last of the Pawnee tribe crossed the Arkansas River and approached the Pawnee Agency on the bank of Black Bear Creek, ending their trek from Nebraska. In the Indian wars of the 1870s, Pawnee scouts defended Union Pacific Railroad workers as they laid iron across the plains. But the American Government deported the Pawnee and marched them south to Indian Territory (later Oklahoma). The Kiowa had also come from the north; the Cherokee, Creek, Chickasaw, Choctaw, and Seminole from the southeast. The Sak and Fox? The others? The Indian tribes had come from everywhere.

Since 1875, the Pawnee had lived on *administrative callous-ness, official neglect, public indifference.* Once a large tribe roaming the Great Plains, they had dwindled to a few hundred but were now on their way back.

"But the Pawnee had once lived in the area," Bix had told Edith. "The removal was a return to land they had once occupied."

A replica of an earth lodge faced east on the Pawnee Agency.

What happened to a people used to hardship when they began to regain strength? What would they do without the struggle that had become a part of them and left an emptiness when they no longer had it? Is that why the lives of Edith and Bill were always torn up? Were they trying to call the hardship back, without realizing it, so their lives would continue with what they were used to? What would they do with the emptiness?

There was the usual in the newspaper. A Pawnee man had killed a white family of four. He was drunk and crossed the center line. There always were things like that in the paper. It kept the Pawnee lawyers busy. The man was not responsible. He had been in the service. He had been wounded, though the exact wound was not clear. He was a part of the Pawnee who honored veterans. But the boys in service got hurt. He had never been the same. He had even counseled young people not to drink. But he had killed while drunk.

Residency

Actually, the world didn't drop off at the edge of Pawnee. Edith drove west on Highway 64 which stretched from Little Rock, Arkansas, to Raton, New Mexico (because Pawnee Bill liked to go to New Mexico). (It was also called the Pawnee Bill Memorial Highway, because he had legislated to build it.)

The land was hilly for awhile on Highway 64 before it flat-
tened to hay rolls in the fields and open country. Edith crossed
the creeks: Black Bear. Lion. Panther. Cow Creek. Bull Creek.
Wolf Creek. The small towns: Lela. Morrison. Then Perry,
where she usually turned south on I-35. It was twenty-seven
miles from Pawnee to the interstate.

This week, Edith did not turn south on I-35 but crossed it,
staying on Highway 64. She continued west across the state on
her way to Goshen, through the counties: Noble, Garfield,
Grant, Alfalfa, Woods, Harper, Beaver, Texas, Cimarron.

The utility poles lined up in western Oklahoma, where the
land was flat as a book. The poles were spidery storefronts
along Highway 64, an invisible town holding the sky off the
empty land. Otherwise the land would be
crushed. Edith saw two corners of a sod   A mask named *Milo.*
house on the flat land. Somewhere on the   A mask named *Silo.*
utility poles, the small, turquoise glass insu-
lators like alien eyes.

What about the people in Goshen? Where would she eat?
Would there be a waitress like Mildred she could talk to?
Would the teachers talk to her? Would anyone ask who she
was, or where she worked, or what she was doing at the
school?

Edith was the invisible one. The visitor. The one who didn't
matter. Here and then gone. But wasn't there something in
that she liked? She had no roots but was free to move on. She
could pack up at the end of the week. They had to stay. Let
my people go, Moses said. (These were the descendants of
Joseph who had gone into Egypt during the famine.) Then,
430 years later (or something like that), they would leave and
return to Canaan. Well, it wasn't that easy. There was Pharaoh.
There was the Red Sea. There were forty years in the wilder-
ness. Making masks. Visiting schools. Getting students to

make their masks. The faces they couldn't be without. It was manna. It was water from the rock. Why did she think church meant nothing to her? What had she named her sons?

A mask moved her from here to there.

Edith thought of her father, J. McKennah, as she traveled. But she thought now she could *drive-through* him. He had had a battle of his own. She could let him go. He couldn't always help her because he was busy with something she hadn't seen. He was only able to be there part of the time. It didn't mean he wasn't with her. And her mother's anger and indifference. She had had her battle too. There was only a part left over from both of them to be parents.

Her sisters, Joanne and Judy, also had their own lives.

Her former husband.

Maybelle was willing to help her as she went on alone. Bix also. Soon the boys would be on their own trail. Were already on it.

The schools, too, had their own lives she touched briefly and then moved on. And the teachers in those schools. And the students. Where would her place be? (In the landscape of her masks. In the hills of noses, in the ponds of eyes, in the opening universe of the mouths.)

Edith had made masks until the inside of the house was COVERED. She kept making masks until the outside of the house was covered. She made masks and masks and masks. She nailed them on the roof of the house. Bix screened in a back porch beneath an overhang on the roof; she filled it with masks. The boys laid a brick floor in the back porch. They used bricks Edith had of her father's; her inheritance. She kept making masks for the backyard, the neighborhood, the sky. God opened the door of heaven, and she kept making masks.

Edith's masks were not aliens from another planet, but from herself. They came from her thoughts. She was still haunted by the alien presence that had had Joseph. It was the imagination more than actuality. How contradictory a human being was. How capable of polarities. A tornado when earth and sky stirred together those strings she could not put her hands through. Disruption in weather. A warm winter day; hail in spring. Love was something you could put your hand through. ◣

Someone betrayed her. The Arts Council called Goshen. Someone in Lawton had complained that Edith was difficult to work with. The clerk in Lawton. Edith knew it. She worked for the state and should remember that she represented the Arts Council. She was responsible for her behavior. She could apologize. Edith hung up.

"Sleep with me, Bix."

"I'd like to, but I couldn't teach Sunday school if I did."

She could bomb the place.

The first night in Goshen was a frog-dark night. ◣

Edith hit the masks as he left.

The students filed into the room the next day. "Name your masks *Uncle Turkey Speed*." Edith started talking, showing them her masks.

She worked Monday.
Tuesday.
Wednesday.
Thursday.
Friday.

Had she had underwear with the days of the week written on them? Her grandmother sent them to her—only her, not her sisters. What had she sent Edith's sisters? Maybe it was Edith's birthday. Had she visited and felt sorry for Edith? Edith the dreamer.

She had worn them out of order. Wednesday's underwear on Tuesday. She liked the rearrangements. She liked to think of Friday's underwear under her pedal pushers on Monday. Her sisters had borrowed them. Sometimes their fights were violent. Her mother despaired. Someday they would be close, she said, but they weren't.

What am I really? How often she heard the students.

Okay. She would work with words. Her masks would lead her exactly where she didn't want to go. Maybe education was the new ceremony.

She walked among the students in the room. "What are the words your mask would say—if it had a tongue?"

Edith saw a student high on something. She saw the spurtz in his eyes.

"What happens to these kids?" Edith asked.

"They work at K-Mart the rest of their lives," a teacher answered. "Their parents take care of them. They get killed in accidents. Sometimes they kill themselves."

Edith thought of the pebbly dirt road where Joanne and Judy had shared a bike. The older sister wearing Edith's Monday underwear.

The spaceship of a teepee rising in air.

A Hershey Kiss.

"It's always Halloween
at your house."

Closing Time

Bill. Bill. It was always Bill. Edith drove through her residencies the rest of the school year. She could push Bill from her mind. Put him behind a mask. But he'd pop out. She could go crazy because of Bill. ◣

Now it was summer.

What would Edith do with herself until school started again?

Bill had married Joel Thomas!

What?

Edith heard it from Maybelle.

MARRIED?

Yes, Benjamin agreed. It was true. Joseph and his girlfriend had stood with them.

"Is Joe married?"

"Not yet."

Suddenly, part of Edith's life was gone.

She got in her car. Drove down the red dirt roads without her masks in the backseat. Drove down the roads she and Bill had covered.

She could not get Bill Lewis back. Had she wanted him back? Would Joseph live with them? Benjamin?

Well, now Edith could marry Bill Bixell. She could learn to trust a man. Yes.

The dirt and pebbles pinged under the car like a hailstorm until she hit paved road on the way back to her house on Nash Street off Fourth.

Edith flew with fury into her workroom. She made a man's mask to wear in front of Bill the next time he came by the house. If he married a woman with a man's name, though it sounded like a woman's, Edith could be a man too. Art was revenge. But when would Bill come by the house? What for? Well, to get the boys.

In a book Edith found a mask! It was a drawing of a shaman wearing a mask that was one like she'd seen in dreams. A shaman in a bird mask flew before a bison wounded by an arrow during a hunt. The shaman was flying to the spirit world to appease the spirit of the dying animal.

There, Edith saw the truth of art. Her masks seemed to

speak at once. They seemed to lift like a flock of birds so thick she couldn't see the walls they hung on. So thick there was hardly room in her house to breathe.

Edith saw her work in the schools as shamans who interceded for others. Who healed. Not her, no, but the work she did with masks. The masks themselves. She was just their driver. How else could she have a job working with something as impractical as masks? She remembered the masks speaking to her in dreams. They went into the schools to ease the burdens of the students, to give them an outlet, if the students let them.

Art was intervention more than revenge, though it could be that, would be that when Edith was requested by ALL the schools in the state, when ALL THE SCHOOLS fought over who got to have her at their school, when HER MASKS were in EVERY SCHOOL in the state, when her MASKS were in the rotunda of the capitol in Oklahoma City, when her masks were the DOME on the domeless capitol.

Her voice seemed to lift the house louder than the flock of squawking birds that her masks were.

QUIET!!!!! she yelled at them.

She was glad Maybelle and Benjamin were gone. She wanted this time alone with her masks.

Masks were invention as well as intervention.

In her arrogance she had thought she was the only one concerned with art; she was the only one who understood. But she was wrong. She had forgotten that art was giving of itself. It was *other* more than *self*. Edith had to be trampled under, too, if she wanted to understand art, and she did. That was how she got to be the Indian Queen. Even if she had to become the Human Pincushion in Pawnee Bill's traveling show. Even if she was a traveling freak show.

The masks taught her that everyone was struggling. She saw

it as she traveled. She was not there to push herself on them as the maker of masks, but as a mask the students could look and see (find) what they needed. If Edith could stand that selflessness, she could be a queen, which to her meant a maker of masks.

Maybelle

You see your son marry another woman. You think the second wife won't satisfy him either. In fact, you think this marriage might be worse. What are you supposed to do? You sit with Benjamin in a church you've not been in before.

How many wives would Bill have? You see them filling his house like Edith's masks.

But there is nothing you can do. You speak as you see him step toward the loss and hurt that is there for him, for them. You try to say, *turn away from the hurt, the loss,* but there is no sound coming from your mouth for your words to ride upon. You see you are a mask. You know how the masks feel. They are mediators. Intermediaries. If only they were understood. But you understand what it is to be a mask. You begin to see what Edith is doing. What the masks are doing through her. You wish you had a mask to wear at Bill and Joel's wedding, though you feel like you're wearing one that no one can see.

You watch Bill and Joel. Joseph and Heather on either side of them. Benjamin beside you on the front row of the church.

You drift from your thoughts back to the wedding a moment, and what you understood seems to blow away. You can't remember exactly what it was you knew, except you sit in the backseat while they drive toward another prison.

Departure

Sometimes Edith was a mask she was trying to take off, if she could get herself out of the way.

"Do you ever stop, Edith?" Bix asked.

She would be happy with Bix. HAPPIER THAN SHE'D EVER BEEN BEFORE.

Maybe the woman who abducted Joseph was one of her masks. Edith lived in a world of those possibilities. ◣

She would open her mask-making business. She would come in off the road: Sure. Edith McKennah Lewis Bixell. EMLB. Masks by EB. Mrs. R&R. Edith Bixell, Mask Maker. Edith McKennah—no, she didn't want to return to that. Bixell's Masks. *Surpassing in Truth and Intensity. The Amusement Triumph of the Age.*

Maybe the masks required her to be willing to sacrifice her son. No, that was the story of Abraham and Isaac.

Yes, it was a one-story world.

Joseph and Benjamin would find their places in Pawnee, or somewhere like Pawnee.

Bill would move into the distance like one of the trains Edith watched disappear down the railroad tracks.

The Indian Queen

Cameron University in Lawton called Edith in midsummer. They were performing a play in the fall. It required masks. Could she come and advise? Could she come and possibly design? Possibly help make the masks? They weren't sure yet.

The students were required to do some of the work. But they needed guidance.

The university would pay Edith's way, provide housing and meals in the dormitory. There would be a small stipend. That was all for the moment.

Where did they get her name?

Eisenhower High School. One of the drama instructors at Cameron had a daughter at Eisenhower. She'd been in Edith's class. Principal Potifar also recommended her. Was Edith coming back to Lawton in the fall?

Yes, but MacArthur, not Eisenhower. How long would they need her in the summer?

Possibly a few days. Maybe a week if they got into the construction of the masks. Could they send the script? Edith could read the play and think about the masks? There were designs for masks suggested with the script, but they didn't like them.

When do you want me to come?

Mid- to late August. When are you at MacArthur?

Edith checked her book. Late September. But only a week.

The play was the first of October. Maybe she could come back for it. But she had another residency that week in another part of the state.

Edith hung up the phone.

What had fallen out of the sky? A phone call. A simple ringing of the phone. Changing her world. Bill had gotten married. Her masks would be on a stage in Lawton, Oklahoma. Her long residency at Eisenhower High School had not been for nothing after all.

Maybe other colleges would hear about her masks.

Maybe she (the Indian Queen) (the Maker of Masks) was on her way at last.

Thĕ Masks

Edith was walking down the street in Pawnee, finishing errands before she left the next day, when she saw BILL and JOEL LEWIS!!! Walking toward HER!! They were with JOSEPH, Heather, BENJAMIN, and MAYBELLE. Going to Mae Lillie's for supper Bill said how are you fine and you Benjamin hello Edith said as if she were a stag or yak or arctic polar bear or panther or the Big-footed Boy from Pawnee Bill's Wild West INTERGALACTIC SHOW. She wanted OUTER SPACE!! WHERE COULD SHE GO? At least they didn't ask her to join them. GET HER OUT OF HERE!!! She was never coming back to Pawnee. Nice seeing you yes enjoy your supper. Trip on the step. Choke on a chicken bone. She was going to have to find some other place to live. ◣

She saw it now. The car was a mask with two headlights for eyes. The travel, also, was a mask that hid her. She wasn't always sure where she was going, but she was going.

She was FURIOUS that she saw the boys with Joel Lewis. Was her relationship with Joseph and Benjamin threatened? That's what she felt! Joe and Ben were Edith's boys. They would always be hers. But they were with Bill, too. Would they stay with him? Was that the price Edith paid for traveling with her masks? No, a new wife did not like the former wife's children. If they decided to live with Bill, they would return. But they hadn't left. Their things were at Edith's house. They were still her boys.

She was a Maskalator.
She was Maskador.

How necessary driving was. Was she just now realizing?

There was a road above the road where she could sort through her thoughts. She was on it.

She would call the boys as soon as she got to Lawton.

A mask was a story.

A mask was a mask.

A mask was a fabrication, which meaning was. Maybe masks were closer to words than Edith thought.

A mask was a state of observation, interpretation.

A history. A lie.

A mask was a house. A mask was a storehouse (of memory).

A mask was an uncertainty.

A mask was something clear: a customhouse you passed through for permission, for an accounting of, for clarity, direction, for setting records straight.   A mask was a welt.

A mask was a stall.

Edith was back to the teacher in the first grade or second or third or fourth who had pinned her mask beside the childrens' masks to show them what they couldn't do. Edith was struck with the failure of her efforts in the face of the face of her masks. She was still reaching.

The Maskalator laughs.
The Maskalator does not give up.
The Maskalator is independent.
The Maskalator is responsible.
The Maskalator does not show what it feels like to be a mask.

But the closer she reached, the farther away she got.

Edith watched the rush of smoke across the road (from a nearby brush fire).

Holy. Holy.

Whatever was going on, Edith picked up on it. She saw it through her masks.

Was she dreaming?

As Edith drove, the sky OPENED UP. There was trampling; a STAMPEDE of herds. Heaven was on FIRE. There was a brush fire in space. She drove on the highway as if going somewhere, but she was stuck in space. Her vision of masks was her subject, her rider. She saw HORDES of masks. She saw a burning-back of brush in heaven. Only she was the brush being burned. Were her masks on fire? She tried to turn to the backseat, but there was smoke and she couldn't see. She was in a stampede, yet she was a bystander. She was ALL RIGHT. It was the stories she heard in church she carried with her. Is that what the minister had said? Or was it Bix? She was watching the herds of heaven. That's what they were. Mounting up, RIDING INTO BATTLE across the earth. Was it the LAST TIME EVIL was loosed again? Maybe not yet. Somehow she drove on.

> Every time the bucks went clattering
> Over Oklahoma,
> A firecat bristled in the way.
>
> WALLACE STEVENS,
> *"Earthy Anecdote,"* 1918

Fangs of flames from prairie fires were eating the sky, were eating the air until she couldn't breathe—only it was as if she were the flames and air was all the things that stood in her way, and she was suddenly eating all the impossibilities and all the barriers she had ever known.

The mask was a new definition of an old subversion. Edith could put the blue fireball of her heart in a mask and get lost and no one would know where she was.

Oh *holy, low rolling hills of fire.*

Edith drove on in the mask, which was her car, past the place where the road had stopped or turned to gravel, and the mask, with its white eyes that could see at night, was full of unbelievable mystery on the road ahead.

Had not Joseph sat in prison in Egypt with the storehouses full of grain that would feed the world as it was then known before him? Weren't they there, though he didn't see them as yet?

Edith could have parlayed the evening's edge into a table-cloth in Dothan's Cafe, or Spurvey's, or any of the cafes where she had eaten during her residencies—all the tablecloths lifted to the sky as a squall line along the horizon. A frantic zip of open sky zipped up again after its spill of rain, up the hood of her car and over the windshield with the wipers beating fran-tically to clear the way. A burst of rain as if from some Friday-night game above. The meeting of two winds swinging tornado like across the field of her windshield.

Was there smoke from a prairie fire, or was it tornado winds that swept past her on the road? Could it be both? Was she in a vision the old people still had? She wasn't dreaming. No. She was still on the road. SHE WAS THERE TO STAY. The schools could get used to her. They could rewrite their history to include her Indian/part-Indian history. Edith had started behind, far behind. She was now on the road ahead. The tornado of her will alone propelled her. Her vision, her masks, the way she saw them, made them, explained them, got others to make them also. She was a manifest destiny of her own making. America, move over. She could take the defeat handed her, some of it by her own hand, and turn it around. She was no longer marked, absent, tardy, disin-terested, disappearing.

In a mask, Edith flew into U.S. Air Force high altitudes.

In a mask, Edith had a respira-tor for thin air.

She had to have a mask. Other-wise, she would scare them with her vision that cut open the world and exposed its hot core.

Write seven times on the board:
I will not let my face show.
Will not let my face show.
Not let my face show.
Let my face show.
My face show.
Face show.
Show.

In a mask, Edith saw the earth was a tiny ball that kept its door shut so she could fly its hot, curved surface as it went around the awful, awesome universe.

In a mask, Edith saw the earth, itself, was a mask.

A mask was an understatement.
A mask was the bit in a horse's mouth.
A mask closed the open seam of the world.
A mask was the seam of the world.

YAWEH: Grace is the substance of story.

URSET: It is a presence without its mask.

YAWEH: Or perhaps a mask behind which there is no presence.

URSET: There is nothing?

YAWEH: A mask of words behind which there is nothing, only silence.

URSET: Grace.

In the Bear's House
N. SCOTT MOMADAY

ACKNOWLEDGMENTS

The ideas for Maybelle's stories of the masks are from "Origin of the False Face Company, Seneca Myths," collected by Arthur Parker, in *Native American Literature: An Anthology*, edited by Lawana Trout. Lincolnwood, Ill.: NTC Publishing Group, 1999.

Excerpt from *In the Bear's House* by N. Scott Momaday, copyright © 1999 by N. Scott Momaday, reprinted by permission of St. Martin's Press, LLC.

Acknowledgment also to *Mask, Faces of Culture*, an exhibit of masks at the St. Louis Art Museum, St. Louis, Missouri; The Buffalo Bill Museum and Ranch, Pawnee, Oklahoma; The National Museum of Women in the Arts, Washington D.C., where I first read from the manuscript, January 28, 2000, and worked with high-school students again.

Special acknowledgment to the State Arts Council of Oklahoma.

Acknowledgment to Twana Turner's third-grade class, Tuscumbia Elementary School, Tuscumbia, Missouri, for their work on masks and poems, October 27, 2000. The poem "Myself" by Kara Rowden from that class appears on page vii. Excerpts from poems by Ms. Turner and by Tyler Hicks appear in the text.

Gratefulness to Mark Anthony Rolo, who said, *Write about it.*

9 780806 191942